D0722383

Nick and the Glimmung

Nick and the Glimmung

PHILIP K. DICK

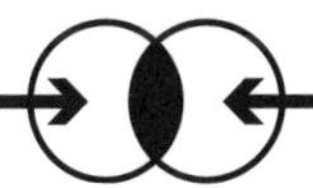

Subterranean Press 2009

First US Edition

ISBN
978-1-59606-168-2

Subterranean Press
PO Box 190106
Burton, MI 48519

www.subterraneanpress.com

List of Illustrations

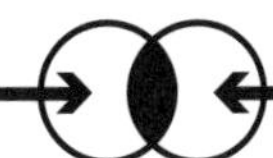

Chapter 1

NICK knew exactly why his family intended to leave Earth and go to another planet, a colony world, and settle there. It had to do with him and with his cat, Horace. Owning animals of any kind had, since the year 1992, become illegal. Horace, in fact, was illegal, whether anyone owned him or not.

For two months now, Nick had owned Horace, but he had managed to keep Horace inside the apartment, out of sight. One morning, however, Horace climbed through an open window; he scampered and played out in the back yard which all the apartment-owners in the building shared. Someone, a neighbor perhaps, noticed Horace and called the anti-pet man.

"I told you what would happen if Horace ever got out," Nick's dad said, after he and Nick managed to round up Horace and bring him safely back into the apartment.

Nick said, "But it's okay now. We found him." He was out of breath from chasing after Horace. The cat, on the other hand, seemed calm, not winded at all; Horace seated himself in his accustomed spot before the living room heater and began to wash.

"It's not okay at all," Nick's father said. As usual, he was tense and worried. "The anti-pet man will be here within the next forty-eight hours. He'll not only make us pay a fine—he'll also take Horace away."

Nervously, Nick's mother asked, "Will the fine be very much, Pete?"

"I don't care about the fine," Nick's dad said. "I care about them taking Horace away; that's what I care about. I don't think they should take a child's pet, or any other pets. I realize that food is scarce, these days. I know why the anti-pet law was passed. But a cat doesn't eat that much."

"It's the law," Nick's mother pointed out. "We have to obey the law, whether we approve of it or not."

Nick's father said, "We can leave Earth. Go to another planet where it's legal to have pets. And not only pets—we could also raise sheep and cows and chickens, whatever we wanted."

A strange feeling came over Nick when he heard his father say this, because he knew, by his father's tone, that he was serious. His father was actually considering leaving Earth, as he had a number of times during the last two years.

For a long time now, Earth had been terribly overcrowded. Too many people existed now, more and more of them each year. No one lived in a house any more; that, like owning pets, had become illegal. People here in San Francisco, and everywhere else, lived in giant apartment buildings which rose up floor after floor, and even descended down underground, where families with less money lived. As the number of people increased, food became scarcer; hence the new anti-pet law, and the appearance of the dreaded anti-pet man. Ever since he had found Horace, Nick had been afraid of the day the anti-pet man would come to visit. As his father had often said, it was only a matter of time. Sooner or later the anti-pet man found every animal—found it and took it away.

It was not known what the anti-pet man did with the animals after taking them away.

"I'll take Horace a long way from here," Nick offered. "I'll find someone to take him. When the anti-pet man visits us, Horace will be gone."

"Don't you want to leave Earth?" his father asked. "And live on a colony world, where you can have all the animals you want?"

Nick said, "I don't know." He felt a little scared. To go that far away from home...to a wild place of forests and peculiar creatures. A new world, a different life, a very hard life, everyone said.

Maybe I can ask my teacher, Nick said to himself. Miss Juth can tell me what I should do.

"I won't make you go to another planet," his father said, "unless you actually want to. It has to be voluntary; you and I and your mother, all three of us, have to agree. We must discuss it and consider every detail. We have to think about your giving up school, for example."

"It would be very exciting," Nick's mother said nervously.

The next morning, as he rode the public hovercar to school, Nick planned out what he intended to say.

Since the anti-pet man already knows about Horace, he thought, I might as well talk about him openly in class. I won't have to keep him secret any longer. What would Miss Juth say? After all, he and his dad had broken the law. But he had a feeling that Miss Juth liked animals.

"Good morning, Class," Miss Juth said—or rather her image on the big television screen at the front of the classroom said. Miss Juth, like all teachers, had too many classes to teach. She could not appear in person in any of them. Instead, she spoke to all her students, in all her classes, by means of a TV screen. In Nick's class there were sixty-five pupils, and Miss Juth (as she had told them) taught nine other classes, too. So in all, Miss Juth had about six hundred pupils. Nevertheless, she seemed to recognize each pupil. At least, Nick had that impression. When she spoke to him from the big TV screen she seemed to look directly at him, to see him as well as hear him. He usually felt as if Miss Juth were actually in the classroom.

Nick and the other pupils said, "Good morning, Miss Juth."

"Today," Miss Juth said, "we shall study—" She broke off, then. "I see Nick Graham's hand up," she said. "Nick, discussion period for your class doesn't come until this afternoon. Won't it wait until then?"

Standing up, Nick said, "I have a difficult problem, Miss Juth. It can't wait; I have to ask you about it right now."

"Do you think all the classes would be interested?" Miss Juth asked. "If you think so, I'll turn you on so that you're visible and audible in all the rooms."

Nick took a deep breath and said, "It's about my cat."

After she had recovered from the shock, Miss Juth said, "Good gracious, Nick. I didn't know you had a cat." To all her classes she said, "How many of you knew that Nicholas Graham owned a cat?"

The lights for *yes* and *no* blinked on. In all the classrooms, only Donald Hedge, Nick's best friend, pressed the *yes* button. The tally read: 602 *no*, 1 *yes*, and 11 *undecided*.

"But Nick," Miss Juth protested, "won't the anti-pet man find your cat and take her away?"

Nick said, "My cat isn't a her, and the anti-pet man is coming soon. So that's why I have to talk to you right away."

To all her classes, Miss Juth said, "How many of you think that the anti-pet man ought to take away Nick's cat? Let's see your votes." This time *265 no* lights came on and 374 *yes* lights. "The majority of the students," Miss Juth said, "think you ought to give up your cat, Nick, and obey the law. Which includes, I understand, paying a fine."

"My dad," Nick plunged on, "thinks we should emigrate to another planet. Where we can keep Horace."

"What an interesting idea," Miss Juth said. "Very original and I would say very brave. Well, children? How do you feel? Let's all of us vote as to whether Nick and his family should emigrate to another planet."

In Nick's classroom a hand went up. It belonged to Sally Sedge. "What does 'emigrate' mean, Miss Juth?" Sally asked.

"Nick, can you tell Sally what 'emigrate' means?" Miss Juth said.

"It means go to live there," Nick answered. "Not just to visit but to stay."

"I see," Sally Sedge said. "That's interesting to know."

"And now the vote," Miss Juth said, "as to whether Nick's father is right in deciding to emigrate from Earth."

The votes read: 189 *no* and 438 *yes,* plus a number of *undecideds.*

"The children agree with your father's decision," Miss Juth said. "However, I must cast my vote; which, as you know, is decisive." She pressed a button on her desk. All the *yes* lights winked off. Miss Juth, by voting *no,* had cancelled them out of existence. "I am against your emigrating, Nick," she explained, "because there are no proper schools on the colony worlds. It would disrupt your training; you would never be able to get a job."

Nick said, "But I can't give up Horace."

A hand went up across the aisle from Nick; it belonged to his pal Donald Hedge. "Maybe," Donald said, when Miss Juth pointed to him, "maybe Nick could become an animal doctor."

"But we don't need any animal doctors on Earth," Miss Juth pointed out, "since there are no longer any animals."

Donald Hedge persisted, "He could be an animal doctor on the colony planet he emigrates to."

"I just don't know, " Miss Juth said doubtfully, shaking her head. "Maybe you're doing the right thing, Nick; maybe I'm wrong. I just don't feel that a cat is important enough to cause you and your family to change your entire way of living, in fact to leave Earth completely. Your father will have to give up his job, for instance. Had you thought about that?"

Nick had a ready answer for that. "My father," he said, "is not happy at his job. He feels he's not accomplishing anything. All he does there is—"

"I'm sorry," Miss Juth said, interrupting Nick, "but we must turn to our first topic of the day, which is a vital one. How Does One Fight His Way Aboard a Bus? we are to ask ourselves. Boarding a public hoverbus is difficult, even for adults, since these days so many persons want to get on a particular bus at a given moment. Press button A on your desk, and the written material on this topic will emerge. Meanwhile, on the TV screen you will see what can go wrong in bus-boarding. It could happen to you, just as it is happening to the man shown."

Leaning towards Nick, Donald Hedge whispered, "I think it's very fair to your cat. For you to emigrate, I mean. And look at all the *yes* votes you got. Most of the kids agree."

A robot monitor standing in the corner of the classroom said in its tinny, loud voice, "No talking."

"And," Donald finished, "you wouldn't have to go to school. At least not this kind of school, where you just see your teacher on the TV screen. Where you don't really get to see her or talk to her in real life. And she's told us she has nine other classes."

Nick said, "I like school. And I always have the feeling that Miss Juth really sees me and is talking directly to me."

"An illusion," Donald said, in a tone of voice that showed he knew—or thought he knew—everything.

"I will call the police," the robot monitor threatened, "unless the talking ceases." The robot monitor always said that, Nick knew;

it was a recording that played from deep within the machinery of the monitor. It never actually had called the police, not in all the years he had been in the same classroom with it.

Do I really want to go to another planet? Nick asked himself as he pressed button A on his desk. Is it worth it, just to keep Horace?

A good question. And, at the moment, one which he could not answer.

Chapter 2

THAT night, when Nick got home from school, he found a tall, dark-haired man, with a briefcase, waiting in the living room. Nick had never seen the man before.

"Are you the anti-pet man?" Nick asked, feeling his heart thud in fear. He looked around for Horace but saw no sign of him. Maybe the anti-pet man had already snatched up the cat; perhaps right now Horace was inside the briefcase. However, the briefcase did not bulge, so it was not likely.

Nick's mother, from the kitchen, said, "This is Mr. Deverest, Nick. He's from the newspaper. He wants to interview your father." Drying her hands she came into the living room. Her face shone with excitement. "They're going to write about Horace's situation and what can be done about it."

"How did you know about Horace?" Nick asked Mr. Deverest.

"We have secret ways," Mr. Deverest said pleasantly. He looked here and there in the room, one grey eyebrow raised. "I don't see the cat. Is he outside?"

"Mr. Deverest is going to take pictures of Horace," Nick's mother said. "To awaken public sympathy for him."

"Is the cat outside?" Mr. Deverest repeated, picking up his briefcase; from it he took a camera and a tape recorder.

"Horace is never outside," Nick said. "Except for yesterday, which was a mistake." He was not sure if he should show Horace to the newspaperman. The less attention that Horace attracted the better, or so his father often said. But since yesterday everything had changed.

"Nick wants to wait until his father gets home," Nick's mother explained to the newspaperman. She put her hand gently on Nick's shoulder. "If Pete says it's all right, we'll show you the cat."

However, at that moment Horace entered the living room. He had heard Nick's voice, and, as usual, appeared for the purpose of greeting him.

"He's not a very large cat," the newspaperman said, with what sounded like disappointment.

Nick said, "You just haven't seen a cat for a long time. Horace is plenty big."

With a sideways glance of mild suspicion, Horace eyed the newspaperman. He stopped and seated himself, not coming any further into the room.

To Nick, the cat seemed large, but in fact Horace was rather undersized. Oddly enough, he had a double chin, a roll of white fur from one ear to the other. Most of him was covered with black—all, in fact, but his stomach and paws and the fluffy white double chin... and, in addition, a white bandit-mask covering the lower part of his face. Horace had a solemn manner, as if he carefully thought every move out before making it...or not making it, as the case might he.

He had unusually long white whiskers which drooped at the ends, giving him the appearance of a wise man, a sage of great age and learning, with little to say; the cat appeared to observe everything, to understand everyone and every event, but to have little to add. He understood but did not comment; he was detached.

At one time—during the first year of his life in particular—Horace had asked a Question. It had been his custom to place himself in front of a person and to gaze up, his green eyes protruding and round, like sewn-on glass buttons, and his small mouth turned down, as if from worry. Staring up, his forehead wrinkled with care, the cat had uttered a single baritone miaow, and then had waited for an answer, an answer to a Question which no one could fathom. What is it that Horace is asking? everybody in the family had said at one time or another. The cat waited each time for the answer to come, but of course it never had. Gradually, over the months, he had ceased asking the Question. But his general bewilderment remained to this day.

Horace now eyed the newspaperman with this traditional concern. It was not a simple confusion; Horace was not asking, Who are you? or Why are you here? He seemed to want to know something deeper, perhaps something philosophical. But, alas, no one would ever know. Certainly not the newspaperman; Mr. Deverest returned the cat's intent stare with uneasiness—a reaction which most people had to Horace's scrutiny.

"What's he want?" Mr. Deverest asked, as if alarmed.

Nick said, "No one to this day knows."

"Can I take a picture of him?" the newspaperman asked.

"Sure," Nick said. But he wished his dad would get home.

Nick's dad worked fifteen hours a week, a special privilege; most people were allowed to work no more than ten hours a week. There were, in the world, certain lucky persons who were permitted to work twenty hours, and, in the case of extremely wealthy or powerful persons, twenty-two hours. To be allowed to work was the greatest honor a person could receive because there were so many people alive now that not enough jobs existed to go round. Many unlucky people had never worked a day in their lives. They filed applications, to be sure; they begged to be allowed to work. They wrote out long accounts of their training, their talents and qualifications. The applications were punch-coded and put into great computers...and the persons waited. Year after year passed, and still no jobs showed up; they waited in vain. So Nick's dad, by present standards, was quite fortunate.

And yet, Nick knew, his dad did not like his job; his dad did not consider it a *real* job, not the sort that people had had in the old days. It was more in the nature of a make-believe job; his dad was paid a salary; he had a desk in an office, but—

"If I ceased to exist," his father had said once, "things would go on perfectly well without me. My job, after my disappearance, could be abolished without doing any harm. Its absence would not be noticed. *My* absence would not be noticed." And he had looked glum.

Nick's mother had protested, "But that's true of most jobs, now! Computers can do just about everything."

"I wish," his father had said then, "that we could live in a world where real tasks, occupations of real importance, still existed. In the old days men called 'craftsmen' made beautiful objects with their hands; they made valuable things such as shoes and furniture. They fixed cars and TV sets. The hands of a man were important, once. Look at my hands." He had held up his hands for Nick and Mrs. Graham to see. "These bands," he had finished, "make nothing and fix nothing. I ask myself, What am I for? Do I exist to do a job? No. The job exists merely to give me the illusion that I am doing something. But what in fact do I really do? Ed St. James, at the desk to my right, examines documents and then, if they arc correct, he signs them. After he has signed them he passes them to me. I make sure that he has not forgotten to sign them after seeing that they are correct. In four years Ed St. James has never made a mistake; he has always signed the documents before passing them on to me."

Nick's mother had said, "But someday he *might* forget."

"And then what?" his father had retorted. "What if Ed St. James does not sign a document? Will our company collapse? Will terror reign in the streets? The documents don't mean anything. They exist to create jobs. One man dictates them. Another man or woman types them up. Ed St. James signs them and I make sure he has signed them. I then give them to Robert Hall, seated at the desk to my left, and he folds them. To his left someone sits whom I have never seen; that indistinct individual places the folded documents in envelopes, if they are to be mailed, or away in the file, if they are to be filed." Nick's father, at this point, had looked very glum indeed.

LOOKING at Horace intently, the newspaperman said in a voice full of doubt, "He doesn't seem very athletic."

This stung Nick to wrath. "How could he be?" he demanded "He never gets a chance to go anywhere outside or do anything. After we emigrate—" He broke off, realizing what he had told the newspaperman.

Both eyebrows lifted. The newspaperman said, "Oh? You're going to leave Earth because of Horace?"

After a pause Nick's mother said, "For several reasons, actually."

"But the cat," the newspaperman said. "That's part of it, eh?" He turned on his tape recorder now. Fiddling with the microphone he said, "Any colony planet in particular, Mrs. Graham?"

"Plowman's Planet," Nick's mother answered.

This time the newspaperman's mouth fell open in disbelief. "Plowman's Planet? But that's so far off. And so wild." Mr. Deverest turned towards Nick and gave him a long, searching look. "Do you realize that an odd variety of animals hangs out there? Animals for whom peculiar names exist names testifying to their unnatural natures?"

Nick said, "Do you always use such long words, Mr. Deverest?" Long words had always annoyed Nick. He knew that much smaller words would do as well, if not better.

"Let me put it this way," the newspaperman said. "It is not cats, dogs and parakeets who live on Plowman's Planet. Cats, dogs and parakeets are simple Earth creatures whom we love and respect. They are attractive and valuable, as for example your cat here." The newspaperman bent down to pat Horace on the head. Horace's ears jumped with distaste, and his whiskers vibrated. "They love us and we love them, even though there is a law against them. What we love, I suppose, is their memory."

"You mean *our* memory," Nick's mother said. "Our memory of animals as they lived in the past. Or, as in the case of Horace, their real but illegal presence."

Speaking still to Nick, the newspaperman said, "On Plowman's Planet you and your parents will meet few other humans. At night when you retire, darkness will settle everywhere. You will see no lights of other houses. No hovercars will zip by overhead. You will have no television set because there is no television. In the morning there will be no newspaper. And as to school—"

Nick's mother interrupted, "We know all this, Mr. Deverest."

"But what about the wubs?" the newspaperman asked. "Do you know about them?"

"No," Nick said. He wondered what a wub was. From the name he imagined it: large and round, with short legs and moth-eaten hide, a large flat nose and small eyes.

The newspaperman said, "Wubs live all over Plowman's Planet. As soon as you run across one you will want to return to Earth. A wub is a dull and ugly creature. It looks as if it had no soul. Although inclined to tell long, dull stories, its main interest is in food. It speaks of food; it dreams of food."

"What does it look like?" Nick asked.

"It is large and round," the newspaperman said. "With short legs and moth-eaten hide, a large flat nose and small eyes."

"Exactly what I thought," Nick said. "I could tell by the name."

The newspaperman said, "And in addition there are printers. And trobes. And father-things. There are nunks, Nick. The nunks on Plowman's Planet are well-known to Earth scientists.

They are a war-like creature, but exceedingly small...for which we are glad. And a nunk is not very bright. We are glad about that, too."

"I think I've read about the nunks," Nick said. But actually he hadn't. By saying this, in a calm way, he wanted to show the newspaperman that he was not afraid.

"And the spiddles," the newspaperman said. "What in heaven's name are you people going to do out there among the spiddles? Think about it before you answer. It is true, I have heard, that spiddles are friendly to man, that their real enemy is the werj. It is also true that spiddles—" He broke off, because the front door of the apartment had opened.

A large heavy-set man, wearing a metallic uniform and helmet, whom Nick had never seen before, stood in the entrance. He had a mean, hard face, as if he cared about nothing. As if he lived in a world of ice and iron.

"I am the anti-pet man," he said. And his voice was as cold as dead ashes.

Chapter 3

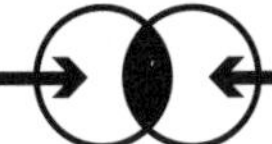

SEEING the anti-pet man, Nick's mother said, "Oh dear." To Nick she said, "I wish your father was home. I was afraid it would happen like this."

In the center of the living room, Horace regarded the anti-pet man in his usual ignorant way. Clearly, Horace did not realize who the anti-pet man was, or why he had come. Such simple questions did not interest him.

Nick said, "Go into the kitchen, Horace. Wait for me there." His heart thudded with greater fear than ever, now. And yet, at the same time he felt calm. It had finally happened: the anti-pet man had showed up to seize Horace. In a way, Nick felt relief. At least the awful waiting had ended.

"So you're the anti-pet man," Mr. Deverest said, as he lifted his camera to take a picture.

"We don't want any publicity," the anti-pet man said in a sharp, grating voice, a voice which perfectly fitted his cruel face.

"I'll bet you don't," Mr. Deverest agreed, and took a picture of him. "Now, let's have one of you stuffing Horace into that cage you're carrying. And then one of—"

"I am not taking the boy," the anti-pet man said. "I am taking an animal; to be exact, a cat."

Nick said, "Horace is the cat. I'm Nick Graham."

"Call the cat," the anti-pet man said. Seating himself on the sofa he opened the cage. "It will be easier for everyone if this is done quietly, so as to make as little fuss as possible."

Mr. Deverest snapped a picture of the cage. "Newspaper readers," he said, "will be interested to see this trap for small animals. It rarely happens these days, since so few dogs and cats are left." He aimed his camera at Nick. "Are you going to cry?" he asked Nick. "If so I'd like to get a picture of that, too."

"I'm not going to cry," Nick said.

"It's not a small-animal trap," the anti-pet man said. "It is a healthy, sanitary cage, used for moving the animal from one place to another. No harm is intended." Kneeling down, he held out a small bit of food. "Here, kitty," he said in his grating voice.

Horace stared at him in his customary dense fashion, not understanding what was wanted of him. Or perhaps he was pretending. On many a useful occasion, Horace had managed to appear dense, if it was in his best interest. Nick suspected that Horace knew more than he appeared to know. Horace, like most animals, was clever where his own advantage was involved. As a matter of fact, Horace now began to walk backwards, away from the anti-pet man and his cage. In slow, stealthy movements, Horace was escaping.

"He's going into the kitchen," the anti-pet man said angrily.

"Horace always goes into the kitchen," Nick said. "No matter what the situation. 'When in doubt, eat.' That's Horace's rule."

"His rule of paw," Mr. Deverest said, nodding.

"Pardon?" Nick said.

Mr. Deverest explained, "With a person we speak of a 'rule of thumb,' but cats have no thumbs. So we must speak of a 'rule of paw.'"

Horace, following his rule of paw, moved further back into the kitchen.

"Stop him!" the anti-pet man exclaimed.

"No one can stop Horace," Nick said, "when he's on his way to the kitchen."

From his belt, the anti-pet man brought out a metal tube, which he pointed towards the kitchen. "I shall put him to sleep," he said, "and that will end his illegal activity, his illegal walking backwards into the kitchen."

Mr. Deverest asked, "Since when has it become illegal to walk backwards into a kitchen?"

"For cats, everything is illegal," the anti-pet man said as he aimed the shiny metal tube in Horace's direction. "Walking sideways into the kitchen, for example, is illegal for cats. Walking sideways up the street is especially illegal. Walking forwards into—"

"We get the idea," Mr. Deverest interrupted sourly; he did not seem to like the anti-pet man at all—a feeling which Nick shared.

A voice said, "What's going on here?" Nick's dad stood at the front door, tall and powerful, his face stern. "Who are you?" he asked Deverest, and then he saw the anti-pet man.

The anti-pet man, who a moment ago had seemed sure of his own worth and dignity, looked at Nick's dad and shrank back. "Are you Mr. Peter Graham?" he asked in a wavering voice. "Owner of a cat? Owner of that cat?" He pointed to Horace, who had stopped walking backwards and now sat in the middle of the kitchen, a worried expression on his face. Both Horace and the anti-pet man had the same look about them. Both seemed guilty and uneasy. But of course Horace was usually this way. The anti-pet man, however, seemed to prefer some other frame of mind.

Nick's dad said, "The law says you have to give us two days to rid ourselves of our pet. You can't take him until then." He grabbed the anti-pet man by the shoulder and propelled him towards the front door.

"What a terrific picture this makes," Mr. Deverest said, snapping away with his camera and following after the anti-pet man. "What an ignominious end to a functionary of officialdom."

The anti-pet man stood awkwardly by the door.

"What does that mean?" Nick asked Mr. Deverest.

Mr. Deverest said, with satisfaction, "It means that the anti-pet man must obey the law like everyone else. Only in this case he is not pleased. The law works against him."

"Then it's a good law," Nick's mother said.

"It's a good law," Mr. Deverest agreed, taking one more picture of the anti-pet man, "but in two days another law will be on his side."

"But in two days," said Nick's father, turning towards them, "we will be on our way to Plowman's Planet. And Horace will be with us. In outer space the anti-pet man will have nothing to say; his law will cease. A new law, the law of reality, will protect Horace for years to come."

Mr. Deverest said, "Unless a werj eats Horace." To Nick, he went on, "I forgot to describe the werjes that exist on Plowman's Planet, along with the wubs and the printers and all the rest. I understand that werjes have a particular—"

"Plowman's Planet," Nick's father broke in, "does not merely mean the danger of being carried away by the wild winged werj. I know of the werj; I know of other dangers, too, both to us and to Horace. But Plowman's Planet means forests and an expanse of great, rolling meadow. It means a place in the shadowy green for Horace to play unseen. There are lands of pasture, fields of mice. There are rivers that roll down to the sea. We will live among the grass; Horace will hunt under an amber moon which lights up cliffs and the hollow places. Fruit, plucked by our own hands, will lie heavy in the woven baskets of our lives. We will plant and farm; we will reap; rain will wash us and the bright sun of day will—" He paused, thinking. "Will do whatever it is a sun does. The usual thing."

You have dreams," the anti-pet man said wistfully, stepping forward, "such as I never have."

Nick's father asked, "Don't you ever dream?"

"I dreamed once," the anti-pet man answered. "I dreamed I was a baseball, in a game between the Giants and the Dodgers." He became silent, then. Everyone waited, but he remained silent.

"What happened then?" Nick asked.

The anti-pet man said sadly, "I was thrown out of the game in the top half of the first inning. What happened next I forget; there is a curtain in my mind which bars all that from my memory."

"Come with us," Nick's mother said to the anti-pet man in a kindly voice. "You will dream dreams which you never suspected. By that I mean: you will cease to be an anti-pet man and your real nature will show itself. You will blossom like a—" She thought for several moments, wanting to say the right thing.

"Like a horned klake," the anti-pet man said, in his usual grating voice. He had lost the gentleness which, for a moment, had come over him.

"What is a 'klake'?" Nick asked him. He did not like the sound of that name; it suggested slithery things which crawled in deep water, out of the reach of men and the light of mid-afternoon.

The anti-pet man said, "There are horned klakes on Plowman's Planet. In an instant, one of them could snatch up your cat and carry him to a rocky peak, amid bones and the dead feathers of things already eaten. They are the enemies of all."

"Be quiet!" Nick's father said harshly, and his face turned red with anger.

"He's right," Mr. Deverest said. "About the klakes, I mean. There are admittedly a very few klakes on Plowman's Planet; we did a feature article on them, once. They were greatly to be feared, then. But not so much of late."

"We're not afraid," Nick said, fighting down his bit of fear, his own personal small amount of it. "Anyhow, Horace knows how to hide. He can make himself almost invisible."

"Horace blends," his father agreed. "He can make himself amazingly indistinct, when the situation calls for it." Eyeing the anti-pet man with dislike he said, "Look how long Horace eluded you."

"Goodbye," the anti-pet man said in a gloomy voice. The front door closed after him.

"He's gone," Nick's mother said. "But he'll be back."

Putting one hand on Nick's shoulder and the other on his wife's, Mr. Graham said, "But we won't be here. It's already been decided; today I booked passage for the four of us on a ship leaving the Solar System for Plowman's Planet. Tonight we've got to pack. We'll have to hurry."

"By 'the four of us'," Mr. Deverest said, "do you mean to include me? I ask that because I don't think I can come along. For example, I have to—"

"I referred to my family," Nick's father said. "To me, to my wife, to my son and to our cat." He turned to Nick. "Make sure Horace has all his things, his dish and his collar and his food. Make sure he has his sandbox and his bed and the catnip mouse which we got him last month but which he never uses."

Plowman's Planet, Nick said to himself. I wonder what it'll be like? Well, he would soon know.

"I'll get all of Horace's things together," he told his father.

"And your own, too," his father said. And he looked at his watch to see how much time they had left before the ship took off.

Chapter 4

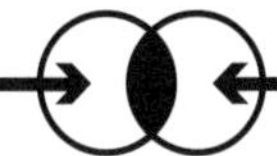

By hovercar the four of them rode to the space port, where their ship waited. Nick found himself shivering with excitement. The great ship, sitting on one end, rose up against the sky like a fat bottle. Wisps of vapor rose from its engines. Here and there tiny human figures worked.

Horace seemed to Nick to have a strange reaction to the sight of the great ship. Although surrounded by his possessions, the cat gloomily shrank within himself, as if offended. Horace paid no attention to the job of transferring all the cartons and boxes from the hovercar to the ship; instead, he fished for a bit of pencil which had fallen into a crack.

Nick's father said, "Cats resist travel. This is true of almost every cat, although now and then you will read of one joining a circus or floating out to sea on a cake of ice. Horace will be all right."

Soon they had all their things aboard the ship.

"This is the last day of our life on Earth," his father said as the four of them were strapped into their special seats. "We shall not see its like again," he added sadly.

The crewman strapping Horace pulled the straps too tight. In a flurry of outrage Horace bit him.

"Easy does it, Horace," Nick's dad said.

"He doesn't want to go," Nick said.

"True," his dad admitted. "But after we get there he'll approve of it. Cats take a dim view of any change. They have what is called a high inertial quality, or rather an introversion of their psychic attitude."

"What does that mean?" Nick asked.

His dad replied, "It means nothing at all. It was just a random thought that came into my mind." To a passing crewman, he said, "How long will it be before we reach Plowman's Planet?"

"We haven't taken off yet," the crewman said, and went on by.

"I know we haven't taken off yet," Nick's father said to Nick and to his mother. He looked even more worried than usual.

"Easy does it, Pete," Nick's mother said, with a smile.

"What I've got," Nick's dad said, "is what is called a high inertial quality, or, as it is sometimes called, an introversion of my mind. It's something I can't help. I'll feel better about it after we've been there a while. But right now—"

"Cool it, mac," a crewman called as he made his way up the aisle between the seats. "You're scaring the cat."

Nick's dad said grumpily, "I am not known as a person who causes fear to arise in cats."

From a loudspeaker at the far end of the ship, a voice boomed, "Take-off in two minutes, ladies and gentlemen. Make sure that you are strapped in tightly. If you have an animal with you, a dog or a cat or a parakeet, hold on to it with both hands, because it has been our experience, over the years, that a dog or a cat or a parakeet slides out of its straps during take-off. And, because of this, they are known to fall on their nose."

The huge engine of the ship roared on. The ship vibrated.

"Here we go," Nick's dad said loudly, over the roar.

At this important moment, Horace had a coughing fit. Eyes shut, head down, he coughed and coughed.

"Horace," Nick's dad said reprovingly, "do you always have to have a coughing fit when something major happens?"

On and on Horace coughed, without looking up. Or answering.

Like released thunder, the ship climbed into Earth's morning sky.

THE trip took ten days. Nick spent most of his time in the ship's games-room, playing ping pong with an electronic adversary who never missed. His mother and father watched entertainment tapes, and, when that bored them, educational tapes which told all about their destination.

Horace, when released from his chair, hid in the laundry room. Nick lured him out with a ping pong ball, which Horace played with during the long, empty hours.

I hope it's more exciting than this on Plowman's Planet, Nick said to himself several times.

"Miaow," Horace said, waiting for the ping pong ball to be rolled towards him.

Since leaving Earth, a strange change had overcome Horace. When not playing with the ping pong ball, he sat staring at the wall of the ship, as if expecting something to emerge from it. Maybe he hears something, Nick thought once. Something outside the ship which Horace thinks is trying to get in. And, after the sleep period, Nick sometimes found Horace high up on a shelf in one of the supply cupboards. Horace, at such times, seemed deep in thought. He sat with his front paws tucked under him, and his eyes...round and large, they were. Not like the eyes of a cat, but more like human eyes, except, of course, for the fact that they were dark green. And at these times, Horace's mouth turned down, like a little old lady's.

"Horace," Nick said to him, one time, looking up at the high shelf on which Horace sat, "you must adapt yourself to new conditions. Things can't always be the same. We all must adapt ourselves, my dad included."

His eyes large, his mouth turned down, Horace stared at Nick in silence, no part of him moving, not even his tail.

"We're pioneers," Nick told the cat. "My dad says we'll clear the land and plant crops. You can ride on the plough, Horace; you can tell my dad which way to go." He waited, but the cat did not respond. "You can chase wubs," Nick added hopefully.

Horace gazed down at him. Silently.

"Printers," Nick said. "You can chase printers." Horace said nothing. Nor did he stir.

"Trobes," Nick said.

Slowly, Horace shut his eyes.

"Father-things," Nick said.

Horace settled down for sleep.

"And nunks," Nick said loudly, to wake Horace up. "And spiddles, Horace; what do you say about the spiddles? That's the real question; what about the spiddles? Think about that."

Horace opened his green eyes, wide and round. And his mouth turned down even more. He looked very worried, and not a bit self-composed. Clearly, spiddles worried him.

"You're going to need our help," Nick said to him, "in combating spiddles. So don't be aloof. Don't plan to rely on your claws and your clever cattish evasive tactics." He had heard his dad speak this way to Horace, and it always seemed to promote the right attitude in the cat—for a while at least.

Coming up behind Nick, his mother said, "There's no use trying to reason with a cat, any cat. He'll have to find out for himself."

"You'll come flying to us for help," Nick said to the cat, "as soon as the first spiddle tries to carry you off."

Once more Horace's green eyes began to close. But not entirely. Uneasily, Horace continued to watch him, and to listen.

The voice of the ship's captain suddenly boomed from the loud-speakers dotted here and there in the ship. "Ladies and gentlemen, we will soon be setting down briefly at Plowman's Planet, where we will discharge three passengers and a cat, pick up mail and food, and make certain minor repairs. Please reseat yourselves and strap in tightly."

"We're there," Nick breathed, hardly able to believe it. "Come on, Horace," he said. "Back to your seat."

Chapter 5

BELOW them an orange world hung amidst mists, as if steaming in the light of its nearby sun.

"It looks alive," Nick's mother said, and shivered excitedly. "Orange forests; how odd. They didn't mention that in the educational tapes. I suppose they forgot to."

"The orange," Nick's dad explained, "comes from the fact that most of the plant-life on the planet is silicon-based in its metabolism, rather than carbon-based."

Nick knew what that meant, or thought he did. "But carbon-based plant-life will grow there," he said to his dad.

"Yes," his dad agreed. "We're bringing wheat seed and the seed of various vegetables, which we will plant, and which will grow far larger than on Earth, due to certain properties in the atmosphere."

"Cool it, mac," a crewman said, passing by their seats. "You're confusing the boy and scaring the cat."

Nick's dad said sternly, "I do not confuse boys." With a low rumble from its retrojets, the ship backed down to a soft landing on the surface of the planet. Looking out of the window Nick saw distant trees and tangled, yellow bushes. And, at the edge of the flat landing-field, a great animal waiting.

"A wub," Nick said aloud, and his heart raced.

The wub had a vast bland face, with a sort of gentle goodness about it. It did not appear to be too bright, but at least it had a kindly look. As the hatch of the ship opened, the wub stumped forward on its short legs, its barrel-like body swaying from side to side. Behind it a foolish and tiny tail lapped, and Nick laughed. So far so good, he decided. This particular life form did not seem harmful at all.

"It's pulling a cart," Nick's mother said, in wonder.

The four of them—Nick held Horace tightly in his arms—walked down the ramp until they stood on the dusty ground. Behind them, crewmen carried their baggage; they set the suitcases and boxes down and counted them. Various packages, stacked nearby, were then taken aboard.

A few minutes later, with a huge and terrible noise, the ship climbed up into the sky, its jets winking with fire. It hung stationary for a moment, then again rose. Nick watched it go until, at last, it disappeared from sight and the noise of its jets died into silence.

We're here, Nick said to himself. He forgot about the ship, and turned to face the wub.

Its crude cart bouncing along after it, the wub stumped forward until at last it reached them. There it seated itself, looking hot and dusty, but friendly.

"Can it talk?" Nick asked his dad.

To the wub, his dad said in a slow, clear voice, "Your cart will hold us all? Including our baggage?"

For a moment the wub eyed him and then it reached into a small bag which it carried about its neck. From the bag it brought a card, which it held up. The printing on the card read:

HOW ARE YOU? I AM FINE. FOR A NICKEL
I WILL TAKE YOU WHERE YOU WANT TO GO.

Nick and his father loaded their baggage into the cart. Then the four of them, with Nick still holding tightly on to Horace, got into the cart along with their possessions.

The wub now produced a second card.

I'D LIKE THE NICKEL NOW.

Nick's father paid it the nickel, which it placed within the bag it carried around its neck. Very slowly, its legs pumping with effort, the wub started off. The cart, with them in it, bumped noisily along behind.

"How will it know where to go?" Nick's mother wondered.

"I'll ask it," Nick's father said. He got out a map of Plowman's Planet, then unrolled and studied it. "Just a moment!" he called to the wub. "I want to show you where our land is!"

The wub halted. It stood resting, looking winded by the effort of pulling them and their possessions. Then, with a groan, it rummaged in the bag around its neck and brought out a third card, which it handed to Nick's father. Nick read it, too. The card said:

NO, THERE ISN'T.

Frowning, Nick's father said, "What does that mean, 'no, there isn't'?" He turned to Nick.

"Maybe it got out the wrong card," Nick suggested.

To the wub, his dad said loudly, "I think you have the wrong card. I said I wanted to show you where our land is.," He spoke the words crisply and slowly, so as to make the wub understand; it did not seem too well supplied with intelligence.

The wub whisked the card back, inspected it, then popped it back into its bag. Quickly, it brought out another one, which it held up for them to read.

I DO NOT HAVE THE PROPER CARD
WITH WHICH TO ANSWER YOUR QUESTION.

"I didn't ask a question!" Nick's father said, with exasperation. "I just want to show you the map!" He held the map out for the wub to see; with his finger he traced the area to which they wanted to go. "See?" he said. "This is the land the U.N. has given us. I understand there's a basalt block house there, plus water, and a certain amount of robot farm-machinery. Can you take us there? Is it far?"

For a time the wub chewed its cud and pondered, and then it rummaged once more in its bag for the proper card. This one read:

I WILL RETURN YOUR NICKEL.

Nick's father said, "I can't seem to communicate with this creature." He turned to Nick. "You try; I give up. Show it the map. Point out the spot I marked."

"Maybe it doesn't understand maps," Nick's mother said. "Maybe it thinks in a different way, not at all as we do; maybe maps have no meaning to it."

"If that's so," Nick's father said, "then I don't see how we can get it to take us to our land. And I don't see transportation of any other kind." He looked upset.

The wub was industriously going through all its cards; it put one after another back in its bag, finally coming down to one, which it presented to Nick, in a hopeful sort of way.

NO, I NEVER GET LOST. NOT IN FIVE WHOLE YEARS.

"It's trying to help," Nick's mother said. "I think actually it's a very good animal, but it just doesn't have enough cards to deal with all the different situations that come up."

"Hand it the map," Nick's father said. "Make it actually take hold of it."

Nick did so. The wub fingered the map—or rather, like Horace, pawed it—and then it ate the map.

The four of them watched in silence, until the last shred of map had disappeared. Then the wub hiccoughed, shook its head as if to clear it, and from its neck-bag brought one more card.

WUBS EAT EVERYTHING.

"Evidently so," Nick's dad said, more bewildered than angry. He did not seem to know what to do, now that the map was gone.

To the wub, Nick's mother said, in a careful and distinct voice, "We have come to this planet to settle. Now that you've eaten our map we have no way of knowing where to go. Can you help us?" She waited, but the wub made no response; it continued to chew its cud nervously, as if wishing to be of help but not knowing how. "There must be other humans near here," she continued, at last. "Could you take us to them?" To Nick's father she said, "They'll be able to help us."

"I think I see some sort of buildings over there," Nick said, pointing. He saw vague outlines against the horizon. "Let's head that way," he said. At least he hoped they were buildings, and if so, made by human beings.

His dad, with a dark and somber expression on his face, said, "I think those are werj dwellings." From the queer, pipe-like outlines of buildings a trail of flickering dots now ascended into the sky.

The wub at once whipped out another card.

WERJES!

"I was right," his dad said. The dots danced towards them, growing larger. There were many of them, a swarm against the late-afternoon sky. Like bits of soot, Nick thought, as if from a twisted chimney. He shivered.

Chapter 6

THE dots came closer and closer until they ceased to be dots. They became winged sails, taking advantage of the wind; they seemed to skim, rather than to fly. Like gliders, Nick realized. Gliders of skin, of black, leathery hide; they seemed to him very old.

"Are we in danger?" Nick's dad asked the wub.

In answer, the wub began to lumber forward. It wheezed as it tugged the cart, an asthmatic noise. Faster and faster the wub ran, but then, all at once, it tripped. The wub fell. The cart teetered, starting to turn over; it swayed, dropping suitcases and parcels on to the ground, and then it came to rest upright.

"Where's Horace?" Nick's mother asked fearfully.

Nick looked rapidly around. Several parcels which had fallen from the cart had split open. Their contents, mostly clothes, lay strewn out beside the cart. He saw this, but he did not see Horace. "Horace!" he said in a loud voice. "Where are you?"

"Under the cart, perhaps," his father said.

The wub had staggered to its short, stocky feet once more. Again it began to run.

Behind the cart, going in the opposite direction, a small black and white shape sped away, as fast as it could go.

"There he is!" Nick yelled. "He's trying to get back to the ship!" Horace doesn't realize it's gone, he said to himself. The ship isn't there, now.

"Turn the cart around!" his dad ordered the wub. "We have to go back for our cat!"

The wub, however, continued on. Behind them, Horace became smaller and smaller; Nick saw only a single point of motion, a black and white spot dwindling with each passing second. Horace had almost reached the place where the ship had rested.

From the sky a werj dropped like a stone, its flapping wings wrapped around itself. It looked to Nick like an ancient umbrella, a dried-up wrinkled umbrella with claws that writhed in the air beneath it. The werj descended a little ahead of Horace, then spread out its sail-like wings. Horace dashed on, directly at it.

"Horace!" Nick shouted. "Open your eyes!" Horace, however, ran on and on, eyes shut.

The werj snatched up the cat and shot upwards once more, to join the other werjes. The pack of them circled now, not coming any nearer to the cart. And yet, Nick saw, they did not go away. They seemed undecided.

"We've lost him," his dad said quietly. His face was pale.

From the pack of werjes, a single werj departed in the direction of the cart. Above the cart it hovered, almost motionless, and very close. And Nick, gazing up, saw it closely—saw into its eyes.

In its eyes he made out infinity, an endless recession of dismal mirrors, within which he himself looked back, his own face, distorted into a mocking mask of sorrow and fright. He saw his own fear, his shock at losing Horace; he saw that warped by the hollow, elderly eyes of the werj, so that it was as if he were taunting himself, for his own worry and concern. And, beyond that, he saw even more. He saw past his own bent reflection. He saw something nameless that leered out from deep inside the werj, not the werj itself but something that lived within the creature, a shape which gasped for air, as if cut off from the world, but wanting to find its way back.

The werj, Nick thought, is only a container. A sort of box. And it has swallowed something awful, which isn't dead, which maybe can never die. He shut his eyes, not wanting to see any more. He had had enough of the werj—and of the creature living out its bloodless life inside it.

Noisily flapping, the werj came to rest on the ground in front of the cart. It said, in a rasping, whining voice, "We have decided to give you back your animal. It offends us; it smells of fish. It smells of the sea. But in exchange for this, we will ask a favor." The werj then let out a sharp squawk, and, overhead, a second, greyer werj swooped down, clattered across the ground on flat, webbed feet, and came to a stop beside the cart.

In its needle-like jaws the second werj clasped Horace.

Horace looked exceedingly angry.

"Let the cat go," Nick's father said.

"There is a war here," the first werj said. "It hangs over the valleys of this world like an evil sticky smoke. By coming here, you are involved in that war, and the favor which we ask of you—that favor concerns the war. We ourselves are part of this war. We have been fighting a long time; we are very tired."

"Just let go of our cat," Nick's father repeated.

"Ask your wub," the first werj said, "if this is so. It will tell you. The wub knows about our great war."

From its neck-bag the wub got out a soiled, much-used card.

YES.

"I see," Nick's father said. He did not look pleased.

Nick said to the werjes, "Could you let Horace go, now?" He could think only of that. In the jaws of the second werj, Horace peered out, looking small and anxious and acutely unhappy.

"Let the creature which smells of fish go free," the first werj said to its companion.

Opening its long jaws, the second werj obligingly dropped Horace to the ground.

Horace scampered away from the werj, but, as usual, in the wrong direction. "Horace!" Nick shouted desperately. "Over here!" Horace, however, continued to run, farther and farther away from the cart. He had seen a tree and he intended to hide in it, as was his custom. "Should I go after him?" Nick asked his father. He started to get out of the cart, but his father held him back with one strong arm.

"Wait until the werjes are gone," his father said. "Then it'll be safe for him to come down from the tree, which he will do, once he knows the coast is clear."

To the first werj, Nick said, "What is it that lives inside you? That awful thing I see behind your eyes?" He did not see it in the second werj, only the first.

The second werj said, "He is aware of Glimmung."

"No one can see Glimmung," the first werj replied sharply. "He is invisible."

"Nevertheless," the second werj said, "he has made out the shape of the wanderer within you." To Nick, it said, "Glimmung has made us old. He will make the world itself old, given enough time. Glimmung is—" The second werj paused, trying to explain what it meant. "The weaver of the web of fate. He has brought this planet's destiny with him, and now it is too late for any of us to escape it."

"Are we included?" Nick asked.

"Everyone is included," the first werj said, or was it Glimmung speaking through the beak of the werj? Nick did not know. "Everyone who comes here," the first werj continued, and its eyes shone like broken, lit-up rocks.

"I will put into your soul," the werj said to Nick, "the memory of Glimmung coming here, back in earlier times. In those days we lived together, trobes and printers, wubs, nunks, ourselves—every life which flourished on this world, including the grass of the fields; yes, even the grass and trees. It was a favored world, a land in which to play, and to be keen about sights and movements, the flicker of the wind which blows across the fields at sunset. We lived in accord with one another, then."

"And then Glimmung came," the second werj said.

"Where did he come from?" Nick asked.

"A star," the second werj said. "A scorched, dead star which had gone out, which no longer burned. There are very few stars as cold as it. The cold ate more and more of Glimmung and at last he left, bringing the cold with him."

The wub, having rummaged within its neck-bag once more, held up another of its printed signs.

HOW ARE YOU? I AM FINE. FOR A NICKEL
I WILL TAKE YOU WHERE YOU WANT TO GO.

"What's that mean?" Nick asked his father. "That's the first sign it showed us."

His father said, "I think it wants us to leave this place and stop talking to the werjes."

"It must be very annoying," Nick's mother said, "to be limited to a few signs for every occasion that may or may not come up."

"It probably has signs it has never used," Nick's father said. "And some signs it uses again and again…whether they apply or not."

Nick said to the wub, "We can't leave until Horace comes down from the tree. And he won't come down until the werjes leave."

The wub brought out another sign.

GOODBYE. IT WAS A PLEASURE TO SERVE YOU.

"It wants us to get out of the cart," Nick's father said, "so it can go on alone." He sighed. "Okay. Come on, Nick; help me unload all the baggage. No use making it stay if it's afraid." He hopped down from the cart and began at once to unload it. Nick did so, too. And presently they had taken everything from the cart.

Nick's mother said, as she stepped down, "It really wasn't much of a help to us."

"But it tried," Nick pointed out. "It did the best it could." He could not blame the wub for being afraid of the werjes. And, after all, Horace meant nothing to it. The wub probably did not even know what a cat was, let alone how valuable and interesting it might be.

The wub lumbered off as fast as it could go, the cart clanking and bouncing up and down behind it. Very soon the wub and the cart had disappeared into a grove of tall orange-colored trees. The sound of its heavy wheezing faded out and then, at last, there was only silence.

"Well," Nick's father said, "I guess we'll have to walk. We'll have to find some other human settlers. They must be around here some place."

The flock of werjes, flying overhead, squawked at the two on the ground. "Come along! Come along! We have business to attend to!"

"In a moment," the first werj said. "Don't tell me what to do," it added. To Nick, it said, "I will reveal to you now the part which wubs have played in the war. When Glimmung came here and took up residence in the High Hills the nunks, who lived close by, wished to leave...but nunks, as you will soon see, cannot move far without help. They asked their friends the wubs to assist them, to cart them away. And this the wubs did—at least for those nunks who could pay five cents."

"Very greedy," the second werj put in. "That is the weak spot in the wub: its greediness. For food and for money, for sleep, for buying and owning as many signs as possible. This is well-known, here on this world. And for it the wubs are looked down on. By one and all."

To his father, Nick said, "I'm going to get Horace." It was clear to him that the flock of werjes would never leave. They liked to talk, on and on; he could see that, now. And Horace had to be rescued now, not later.

"Here is a little book which we have prepared," the first werj said. In his long jaws there appeared a slender volume, and this was waved towards Nick. "A short, official history of the war, prepared by ourselves. It gives a true account of all that has happened, and, most especially, it will protect you from the lies of the Grand Four who fight on the other side."

"'The Grand Four,'" Nick echoed. "Who are they?"

"The printers, first of all," the werj said. "They are the last great enemy of Glimmung. The nunks are almost gone, now, so they do not count; anyhow, they come second among the Grand Four. Third, the human colonists from Earth who live here. They have been misled by the printers, exactly as we hope you will not be misled."

The second werj said, "And the spiddles. They are the last of the Grand Four."

"And the trobes?" Nick asked. "What about the trobes?"

"They are on Glimmung's side," the first werj said. "As are the father-things. Ourselves, the trobes and the father-things—we fight for Glimmung, and one day, we shall win. We have almost won already. Then there will be peace again upon this world, and Glimmung can thrive and flourish; he can grow as he wants to." As the werj said this, something blazed within its eyes. A dull, black fire, like a torch held under water. The spark of Glimmung himself, Nick realized. Residing within the werj, lodged there and smoldering, waiting to come out when the war had been won. He would not wait much longer; Nick sensed Glimmung's eagerness, his horrid need.

"You have told them too much!" the werjes flying overhead cried in their shrill, grating voices. "Let's get away! Leave them and go!" They pumped their wings and started off, back towards the twisted stove-pipe buildings on the horizon.

The first werj dropped the little hide-covered book at Nick's feet, then ran off on its flat feet; it wobbled unsteadily up into the air. It and the second werj rejoined the flock; for a moment they hovered overhead, flying in circles, and then they shot off, as fast as they had originally come. Again they became dots. They had gone.

Nick bent and picked up the dry little book; against his hands its texture was coarse and unpleasant. He read the title. *One Summer Day*, it was called. He leafed through it, glancing here and there at its pages. "This isn't about a war," he said to his mother and father. "It's—" He could not tell; it did not seem to be about anything. Like a book in a dream, he thought. "I don't want to read it," he said aloud.

"I'll take it," his father said. He held out his hand and Nick gratefully gave him the odd little dark volume. "And now you can get Horace," his father said.

Nick ran at once towards the orange-colored tree in which Horace, safe from his enemies the werjes, cautiously hid.

Chapter 7

AFTER they had persuaded Horace to climb down from the tree, and had collected together their scattered luggage, the four of them seated themselves on their mound of parcels and suitcases. "Time for a conversation," his father said. "Perhaps if we discuss our situation we will think of a way out. A way by which we can find our farm, now that the map has been eaten."

Nick picked up Horace and examined him. Since his adventure Horace had become sullen; he glowered with suspicion at everyone and everything. On Nick's lap he sat scrunched down, taking up as little space as he could manage. Clearly, the werjes had offended him; they had snatched him up and then they had caused him to lose his dignity by confusing him, by making him run in the wrong direction. Horace would remember the werjes for a long time; in the future he would keep them in mind, whatever he was doing.

"Horace isn't happy," Nick said. He petted Horace, but the cat sank down, away from his hand. "Maybe if we feed him—"

"This book," his father said, not paying any attention; he held the dark little volume open in the middle, reading it intently. "The werj must have given you the wrong book entirely. This has nothing to do with us. This isn't a text regarding the war."

Nick's mother said, "Maybe the werj lied. Maybe there isn't any war. Maybe it wanted to frighten us. A werj would enjoy that; I could tell." She shivered.

"The wub agreed with the werj," Nick's father said. "So it is probably true." He turned the page and read on. "Hmm," he said aloud. He held the book towards Nick's mother, who took it. "Read the part on the left-hand page. The second paragraph."

"Read it aloud," Nick said, wanting to know what it said.

His mother read, "'When a printer makes a bowl he loses a piece of himself. The bowl grows puddinged. The printer tries harder. But he can't go on. Things taken to him are not printed any longer; the printer is silent. In the end he cannot even print himself.'"

There was a moment of silence as the four of them thought this over.

Nick's father said, "You know what I think this book is? It's a study of the enemies of Glimmung. What they're like and how they can be destroyed."

"Look in the index," Nick said. "In the back." He had a strange feeling, as if he knew what his mother would find. "Look under 'G'. Look for us."

His mother turned to the back of the book. "I don't see how we could be—" She broke off. "Pete," she said to Nick's father, "he's right. We are here. It says, '*Graham, Peter & family*. Page 31.'" She hunted rapidly for the page.

"Read it aloud," Nick's father said in a low, serious voice.

"Here it is." She took a deep breath and read from page 31 of the little book. "'They cannot find their farm. The map has been eaten. The creature which smells of fish misleads them until it is too late. They are undone by their love.'" She paused, her forehead wrinkling. "Our love of Horace, I suppose," she said, finally. Eying Horace, she said, "So we're to blame you because we're lost."

"The werjes," Nick's father said, "are sowing seeds of distrust. They're tricky and clever. This book is a trap." He took it back from her and examined the index himself. "'*Werje*,'" he read aloud. "'Also spelled wurj; more commonly werj. Pages 24 to 29.'" He raised his head. "A lot about them in here. Which isn't much of a surprise."

"Don't read it," Nick's mother said. "I don't think we're very interested in what the werjes have to say about themselves."

Nick's father said, "I don't think the werjes wrote this. I think this is by Glimmung."

"Why do you think that?" Nick asked, wondering how his father could possibly know.

"Listen to this," his father said. He read aloud from the passage in the book dealing with werjes. "'It is a low form which comes from ditches and from cracks in the earth. It uses its skin as a sail. Anything which moves is its prey. Certain intense odors will drive it off. During parts of the year, the summer parts, it can be inhabited, and it will fly everywhere. In the end it will join the horned klake, the enemy of us all. But meanwhile it can be used.'" His father shut the book tight. "A werj wouldn't write that. No creature would write that about itself. Anyhow I doubt if the werjes can write. Neither can the wub. But some life form here on Plowman's Planet can write."

"As you said," Nick's mother reflected. "Glimmung."

"He was terrible," Nick said. "I saw him, down inside the first werj. He looked out at me."

"But he let us go," Nick's mother pointed out. "So he can't be so bad."

"Maybe Glimmung was afraid of us," Nick said.

His father and mother both glanced at him wonderingly.

"A thing can be evil," Nick said, "without being strong. Glimmung may be weak. The war isn't over. There are still printers, at least. And it's afraid of the horned klake. Maybe klakes are even worse than Glimmung." He did not like that idea; it made him very uneasy. The anti-pet man had spoken of klakes. And in a similar way as this book. So evidently it was true.

"What we must do is find the Grand Four," his father decided. "Not another wub; in my opinion the wubs, although meaning well, are of slight value to anyone. Except, perhaps, to themselves; they will, no doubt, survive the war...by being on neither side."

A distant noise reached their ears.

"Look," Nick said, pointing; he saw, far off, a vehicle of some kind, almost like an old-fashioned, ancient car. It pulled behind it a huge vat of some kind, like a water storage tank. How slow it's going, Nick thought. As if the driver doesn't know the way.

"Nick," his mother said excitedly, "run as fast as you can; try to catch up with it. I think I see people in it. Yes, I'm sure I see a man driving it."

Tossing the little leather-bound book aside, Nick's father said, "I guess we have no use for this." He began to wave at the distant car.

"I think we should keep it," Nick disagreed. "We can turn it over to the Grand Four; maybe they can use it." The werj probably shouldn't have given it to us, he said to himself. I wonder how soon it'll discover its mistake. Bending, he picked the book up.

The ancient car had turned in their direction. The driver had seen them. Very slowly the car approached them, taking its time. At last it drew up beside them, making a wheezing noise. Trails of steam drifted up from its radiator.

"Who are you?" the driver asked. "I don't remember ever seeing you before, and I know every colonist on this planet."

Nick's father said, "The ship just let us off. A wub was taking us to our farm, but a flock of werjes scared it away."

"Wubs aren't very brave," the man said. "Where's your farm? Let's see your map."

"The wub ate it," Nick's father admitted.

The driver grinned. "They do that. Do you have your deed? I can probably figure out where it is for you."

From a suitcase Nick's father produced a flat packet, which he opened. He handed the driver an official-looking document, which the driver read slowly and painstakingly.

"Is it far from here?" Nick's mother asked.

"Pretty far," the driver said. "And I'm not going in that direction; in fact I'm going the opposite way."

"But you said—" Nick's father began.

"I said I could tell you where it is," the driver said. "I didn't say I would—or could—take you there." He shifted the gears of his car and it started into motion. "See that mountain peak over there?" The driver pointed. "Keep walking in that direction. Your land is on the near side."

"But our baggage," Nick's mother protested.

"We'll pay you," Nick's father said. "The wub wanted a nickel, which probably isn't enough. But we can pay more than that. How much would you take?"

"Sorry," the driver said as he moved his car away. "Money is nearly worthless, here. What's valuable is water, such as I have in this tank. Water is scarce on Plowman's Planet, as you may have heard." He waved goodbye to them.

Nick, holding up the small book which the werj had given him, said, "Is this worth anything?"

Slowing his car, the driver shaded his eyes and studied the book. "Where did you get that?" he asked. He stopped his car, then.

"We'll trade it to you," Nick's dad said, "if you'll take us and our possessions to our land. An even trade. No questions asked."

"No one has ever really seen that book," the driver said. "We thought it was a myth; I didn't believe it actually existed. Sure, I'll be glad to trade you." He shut off the motor of his car, opened the door and slid out. "I'll help you load your stuff into the back."

Nick said, "Why is this book valuable?" His feeling had been correct; the book did have worth, and of a kind they needed.

"That's Glimmung's book," the driver grunted, as he loaded one suitcase after another into the boot of his old car. "Glimmung is supposed to have brought it with him when he came to this planet, years ago." He raised his head, eyed Nick and his parents. "Have you seen Glimmung?" he asked.

"My son has," Nick's father said.

The driver stared long and hard at Nick. "What did Glimmung look like?" he asked presently. "What shape did he take? They say Glimmung can take many shapes. He appears first one way, then another."

"He seemed to be living inside a werj," Nick said. "The werj who gave me this book."

"A werj wouldn't give a human this book," the driver said.

Nick said, "It made a mistake. It meant to give me a history of the war. I don't think it could read."

"True," the driver said. "Werjes can't read. Neither can wubs, although they carry around their untidy little signs." He had loaded the last parcel and suitcase into his car. Now he reseated himself behind the steering wheel and started up the motor once again. "Glimmung will be furious," he said as he held the door open for Nick's mother to get in. "He'll undoubtedly try to get the book back." Uneasily, the driver glanced up into the sky. "We'd better hurry."

The car rolled forward, carrying them towards the distant peak that jutted up from the plain.

Chapter 8

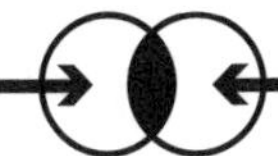

THE sun had begun to set when the creaking old car, with its huge wooden water tank, reached the Grahams' farm. The driver, whose name was Reg Frankis, brought the vehicle to a halt. The five of them sat in silence, gazing at the land ahead.

A flat expanse lay before them, covered with brittle, spiny shrubs, as orange as everything else on the planet. Here and there rested a boulder, and, at one end, an enormous tree.

And the house. Nick stared in amazement at the building. So large a place for them…not like an apartment on Earth. With no other buildings nearby, the house stood alone, a solitary structure which seemed quite solid. Prepared, Nick thought, to last nearly forever.

"Typical government-built house," the driver, Reg Frankis, said. The sight of it did not particularly impress him. Probably all the houses on Plowman's Planet were exactly like this, built by robot work-teams. "Ten acres of land, all flat. There's machinery over there." He pointed. "Farm machinery to plough the land. Elsewhere water is scarce, but you have your own spring." He held out his hand. "Now let me have the book."

Nick's father passed him the little book. Mr. Frankis glanced through it, and, satisfied, put it in the glove compartment of his old car.

"What are you going to do with the book?" Nick's father asked.

"Sell it to the printers," Mr. Frankis said cheerfully. "Now, if you'll unload your things, I'll get started; I have a long way to go, to get back onto my water route."

Nick and his parents unloaded their parcels and suitcases. When the last one had been removed from the car, Mr. Frankis started up the engine and put-putted away. They watched him go until the car disappeared from sight among a grove of spindly trees.

"I wonder how close our neighbors are," Nick's mother said in a small, uncertain voice. "It's so strange, no one living nearby…it makes me…" She gestured. "…feel insecure, I guess."

"We'll get used to it," Nick's father assured her.

Horace had remained quiet during the car trip, but now he all at once became active. He hopped from Nick's arms and trotted off, his tail held low, his head thrust forward as if he were listening.

"Will he run away?" Nick asked his father.

"I doubt it. He seems to know we've arrived." Nick's father began carrying packages towards the house. Nick and his mother helped, and fairly soon they had taken everything inside.

"Almost no furniture," his mother said critically, as she surveyed the empty, echoing rooms.

Nick's father said, "We're lucky they supplied any. In fact we're fortunate that they supplied the house, and the land, and the machinery."

"If they hadn't," Nick's mother pointed out, "we wouldn't have come here."

"Well, there's that," his father said.

Horace, meanwhile, had gone off somewhere. Nick saw him wander into a clump of bushes, briefly emerge, then disappear once again.

A great yowl came from Horace, invisible as he was within the shrubbery.

Nick raced in that direction, his heart hammering. What had the cat found? A creature of Plowman's Planet? He caught up with Horace, whose fur had fluffed out and whose tail had become enormous. Horace hissed, his ears flat, fangs showing; then, seeing Nick, he gave out a plaintive miaow, as if apologizing.

Into the evening darkness a small many-legged shape scuttled, an animal with several rope-like tails. It hurried as fast as it could, then vanished, evidently into a burrow. Horace rubbed against Nick's legs, showing no desire to follow the creature.

"What is it, Nick?" his father called from the porch of their new house.

"A thing that lives here," Nick said.

"Better get inside," his dad called. "We don't know yet which fauna here are harmless and which aren't. Don't take any chances. And get Horace; bring him, too."

At its burrow the many-tailed creature poked up its head, a wary, energetic creature which chattered now, as if signaling to others of its kind. Nick heard scurryings in the nearby bushes; he sensed more of them, whatever they were, answering in agitation, worried by Horace and by Horace's fangs and yowl. Nick said, "It's okay. Horace was just taken by surprise." He listened. The creatures, here and there, continued to chatter. "My cat won't hurt you," Nick said to them.

"You want to bet?" a tiny voice came, from the shrubbery.

Nick said, "He's just a cat. Cats don't hurt anyone."

"Oh, come on," the tiny voice answered. "Don't give us that. Look at those teeth he has. Assassination city. We'll report him to the Grand Four—he's a menace!" The voice rattled with indignation.

"What are you?" Nick asked.

"Spiddles," the invisible creatures said, several of them in unison. "Are you the people who are going to live here?" one of them asked. "And you're bringing that vicious carnivore with you? We'll move out; we'll leave." Others chimed in: "Yes, we'll leave!" The first one added, "That wise-guy cat of yours is riding for a fall. It's either him or us."

"He's part of the family," Nick said.

"Oh wow," the spiddle complained. "Commotion city. Look, mister. We're fighting a war. Have you heard about the war? You *have* heard about the war, haven't you? Have you heard about werjes? Have you heard about Glimmung?"

"Yes," Nick said. It was the first time anyone—or anything—had called him 'mister'. He found he liked it. "I met Glimmung," he said. "And it gave me a book, by mistake. I mean, it intended to give me a book, but not the one it gave me."

"Glimmung gives every newcomer to this planet a copy of *The Last and Final War,*" the spiddle said. "It tells how right they are and how wrong the Grand Four are. There must be a thousand copies of it floating around Plowman's Planet. Lies, all lies."

Nick said, "But that's not the book Glimmung gave me. Or the werj gave me; I couldn't tell which. *One Summer Day,* it was called."

"You have that book with you?" the spiddle asked.

"No," Nick said.

"You lost it. You gave it to a wub and the wub ate it. You made a fire with it. You—"

"We traded it to an Earth colonist," Nick said. "Mr. Frankis. We gave it to him for bringing us here."

"Good old Frankis," the spiddle said, and, in the darkness, its companions chattered with disgust. "Reg Frankis," the spiddle said, "is a thief. Who knows what goes on in his brain? He's what we call a water man; he transports water and sells it at a high price which no one can afford. You've got to get that book back from him."

"Why?" Nick said.

"Because we need it. The Grand Four, in fact, need it. If we're to win the war. Reg Frankis will set so high a price on it that we won't be able to pay. And the Glimmung will buy it back. *They* have plenty of money. We're broke. Poverty city; that's what this is, around here. Why do you think we live in burrows in the ground? Because we like to? I'll tell you why; it's because we can't afford anything better." The spiddle's voice shook with indignation.

"You're lucky," another spiddle, from the darkness, said. "You have that house. All you Earth colonists are lucky. Who looks after us? Disinterest city; that's what it is.

To Nick, the first spiddle said, "Do you suppose you could get that book back from Frankis?"

Hesitating, Nick said, "We made a deal. It's his property now."

"Couldn't you steal it?" several spiddles asked in unison.

"I—don't think so," Nick said. It did not sound right to him, doing that. The trade had been made in good faith.

A spiddle said, "You could have done a great deal to help end the war, to give us a final victory. *One Summer Day* lists the weaknesses of every creature on this planet, trobes and werjes included. Even klakes; no one is missing from its pages. True, the book does tend to drone on, and to stray from the subject… Glimmung's mind is very disordered. But, somewhere in the book, it's all there. Everything—the past and the future. Both."

"And now that profiteer Frankis has it," another spiddle said in disgust. "Bad luck city; that's what this is."

"Bad luck for Glimmung, though," another spiddle said. "To have let the book leave his hands. He must be worried. By now he'll have discovered his loss. Look here, Earth-person; Glimmung will be searching for you, trying to get his book back again. You'd better dig in. Besieged city; that's what you are."

"Tell Glimmung right off," a spiddle suggested. "Say, 'Reg Frankis, the water man—he has your book.' For your own protection. Otherwise it's Vengeance city, Earth-person."

"A rub-out," another spiddle chimed in. "Rub-out city."

"What's that mean?" Nick said. He had difficulty understanding the peculiar speech of the spiddles.

"It means," a spiddle said, "that Glimmung will take you apart bolt by bolt. To find his missing book. Did you look at it? Did you have a chance to read any of it?"

"Only a paragraph or two," Nick admitted. What an opportunity they had lost, he realized. And now it was too late.

"This was once a happy place," a spiddle said wistfully. "Before Glimmung came. He came here slowly, by small, stealthy steps, one after another. There was no particular, exact time when he entered our world. We became aware of him gradually."

"First we heard rumors," another spiddle added. "Vague accounts, nothing definite; the rumors told of something bad, of a wicked thing that existed...but not here. Then, one day, it seemed as if he were almost here, that he had come a little closer. And then we heard from the nunks that he was actually here. And so it went, day by day. The werjes were glad; evidently they flocked to him. And the trobes, of course; they rejoiced—they screamed in the night with pleasure."

"And then we knew Glimmung was everywhere," another spiddle said. "And so we joined with the last of the printers. Because it was the printers that Glimmung wanted most to destroy. We heard that Glimmung bad come to this planet to seek out the printers, that their struggle began before this planet existed. That it was, in fact, as old as time. The printers have never said; they do the best they can, and that is all. They are almost worn-out, our printers; what they make is puddinged, now, very indistinct and almost useless. We pretend, of course, that it's otherwise."

"But it's wise," an additional spiddle added. "Not otherwise."

From within the house, Nick's mother called, "Nick. Time to come inside. You can look around in the morning."

"Goodbye," Nick said to the spiddles. "I'll see you again tomorrow." Excusing himself, he made his way through the darkness towards the brightly lit house.

By the side of the house a clump of what looked like bamboo jutted up. Nick started to pass by it, then stopped.

In the bamboo something grew. A shape, silent and unmoving, that rose up from the soil like some nocturnal mushroom. A white column, a pulpy mass that glistened moistly in the dim light. Webs covered it a moldy cocoon It had vague arms and legs. An indistinct half-formed head. As yet the features hadn't appeared. But he could tell what it was.

A father-thing.

Chapter 9

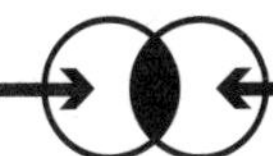

THE father-thing was almost ready. Another few days and it would reach full maturity. It was still a larva, white and soft and pulpy. But the sun of day would dry and warm it. Harden its shell. Turn it dark and strong. It would emerge from its cocoon, and one day when his father came by this spot…

Behind the father-thing were other pulpy white larvae, recently laid. Small. Just coming into existence.

Nick began to move numbly away. Weakly he reached into the darkness, trying to find something to lean on; he felt terribly dizzy and afraid. Turning, he walked a few steps away from the father-thing and the other, newer, larvae—then saw something else. Something which up to this moment he had not been able to fathom.

Another one. Another larva. It wasn't white. It had already turned dark. The web, the pulpy softness, the moistness, all had gone. It was ready. It stirred a little, moved its arms feebly.

A Nick-thing.

"Dinner's ready," his mother called from within the house. "Go and get your father, Nick, and tell him to wash his hands. The same applies to you, young man." Nick could smell food cooking: their first meal on Plowman's Planet.

He made his way into the house, found the kitchen and entered it. His mother was carrying a steaming casserole to the neatly set table.

"What's wrong?" she said when she saw him.

"Something I have to tell Dad," Nick mumbled, still stricken with numbing fear.

"Pete!" his mother called anxiously. "Nick looks really scared; you'd better come in here. You can finish shaving after dinner."

His father, strong and good-looking and alert, strode into the kitchen. "What is it, Nick?" he asked, seeing his son's face.

"Outside the house," Nick said. "I'll show you; come on." He led the way out of their new house, into the night darkness, to the spot where the bamboo-like plant grew—grew with its inner colony of larvae in various stages.

After he had looked at the larvae for a long time, Nick's father said, "These plants are terribly dangerous."

"I know," Nick said.

"It's good you found them in time," his father said. "Another few days—"

"Can we kill them?" Nick asked.

His father said, "I don't see why not." He continued to stare at the father-thing. "I would have been replaced," he said. "By one of it."

"Me, too," Nick said.

"Yes, yours is almost finished. And it looks like you." His father's voice shook. "Exactly like you."

Nick's mother came out on to the porch of their new house. "What is it, Pete?" she called anxiously. "Can I see?"

"No," Nick's father said. "You go back inside." To Nick he said, "If we only had some gasoline. We could burn them up.

"Maybe they're already dry enough to—" Nick began, and then broke off in horror.

The last shred of moist webs had fallen from the Nick-thing. The Nick-thing moved, swayed; it broke itself loose from the base on which it had grown, then tottered out. It floundered uncertainly. Its mouth opened and closed, and then it reached towards Nick.

His father tugged him back, away from it.

"There's a phone in the house," his father said. "We'll go inside and lock the door; I'll call the local police, here on this planet. There must be some kind of way they have for dealing with these father-things."

"Why are they called 'father-things'?" Nick asked as the two of them swiftly entered the house and bolted the door behind them.

"Evidently they usually start out by imitating grown men," his father said. "In this case, however, they were more after you than me."

"Please tell me what's out there," Nick's mother said, coming out of the kitchen with a plate of rolls which she had removed from the oven. "Is it very bad?"

"It's very bad," Nick's father answered. "A Nick-thing. And right outside our new house. How could they have known?"

"In Glimmung's book," Nick said. "It foretold our coming here; remember?"

“That’s true,” his father said. He picked up the receiver of the phone. On the small grey screen the face of an operator formed. “Give me the police,” Nick’s father said gravely.

THE police came very soon, and, outside in the darkness with their flashlights and equipment, they destroyed the bamboo-like growth with its larvae. Afterwards, one of the policemen talked with Nick’s father in the front room of the house. The door was closed, but Nick and his mother could still hear. Nick tried not to, but whole sentences floated to him from beyond the closed door.

“You understand,” the policeman was saying to his father, “that we didn’t get the mature one which had already broken loose. My men are combing this area with infra-red searchlights, but so far I’m afraid they haven’t found it.”

“The Nick-thing?” his father asked. “You mean it’s gone?”

“Exactly,” the policeman said.

“Can you leave a man here to watch for it?” his father asked.

“We’re too short-handed. I’m afraid not. You’ll have to spot the Nick-thing yourself and then call us. They’re easily destroyed; just an ordinary match held to it will burn it up.”

“What would it do to Nick if it caught him?”

The policeman said, “Replace him.”

“But do exactly what with Nick? Kill him?”

Nick could not hear the policeman’s answer. It was spoken very low.

“Is there any other kind of help we can get?” his father asked. “From anyone? Other colonists, perhaps?”

"You have quite a number of spiddles living on your land," the policeman said. "Ask their help. Spiddles are good friends to have; many human colonists have discovered that."

"They would be able to tell the Nick-thing from Nick?" his father asked.

"Every time," the policeman assured him.

The door of the living room opened. His father and the policeman came out, their faces grim.

"Nick," his father said, "as soon as you see the Nick-thing, tell me. Instantly. We'll keep all the doors and windows of the house locked, and you stay inside until—"

"I don't want to stay inside," Nick said. "Anyway if I stay inside I won't be able to persuade the spiddles to help."

"Let him talk to the spiddles," the policeman said. "But during the day time, so he can see if the Nick-thing is trying to creep up on him."

Nick's father hesitated and then said, "What if I or my wife see the Nick-thing? Suppose it pretends to be Nick?"

"That's what it will do," the policeman said. "It'll look like your son; it'll claim to be your son."

"How can I tell the difference?" his father asked. "Suppose Nick goes outside tomorrow morning and then the Nick-thing comes in and says it's Nick?"

"The father-things are not exact or perfect imitations," the policeman told him. "Especially when they speak—they don't say real words; they just make sounds. Talk to it, if you think it isn't Nick. That way, I assure you, you'll be able to tell." The policeman tipped his hat to Nick's mother. "Goodnight. And welcome to Plowman's Planet."

"What a welcome," Nick's father said, as the policeman left and walked across the yard to his parked hovercar.

"I'm not afraid of it," Nick said. And he knew that the spiddles would help, for all their peculiar language.

Horace, who had been exploring the house, now appeared. He seated himself neatly, his great green eyes fixed on Nick.

"To think," Nick's father said to the cat, "we came here because of you." To Nick he said, "It wasn't worth it."

"Don't say that," Nick said. Now that he was indoors, and the police had come and destroyed the thing-bush, he felt much better. True, the Nick-thing was roaming around outdoors in the darkness, waiting to replace him. But—the Nick-thing had seemed fragile to him, and weak. Perhaps it wasn't as dangerous as the other father-things. Anyway, as the policeman said, it burned up at the touch of a match. It was, after all, just a plant.

"I'll say that it wasn't worth it," his father continued fiercely, "until we find the Nick-thing and destroy it."

Nick's mother asked, "Nick, do you think you can strike up a relationship with the spiddles who live near here?"

"Sure," Nick said. "In fact I already have."

"That relieves my mind," his father said. He looked much less worried, now.

In the living room, a fire burned in the fireplace. The house had become warm and friendly, full of the smells of dinner and of crackling logs.

"The spiddles told me what it was like here before Glimmung came," Nick said. "'This was once a happy place,' they told me."

"I believe that," his father said. "And it will be again, when the war against Glimmung has been won." To Nick's mother, he said,

"We didn't know this; we didn't realize, before we came here, that we'd be part of a war that stretches out through the ages. Involving many kinds of creatures."

"The spiddles say," Nick said, "that the war began before Glimmung came to this planet. 'As old as time,' the spiddles told me. Glimmung followed the printers here. It's the printers he most wants to destroy. They're ancient enemies." We'll have to find out where the remaining printers are, he said to himself. And meet them. "The printers," he told his father, "need help. 'They're almost worn out,' the spiddles say. So I guess we'll have to hurry."

"Tomorrow," his father promised.

Horace had gone to the front door; he waited there, gazing up at the knob, as if trying to will the knob to turn.

"He wants to go out," Nick said, going to the door.

Horace continued to gaze forcefully at the knob, still exerting his powerful will in its direction. His will, fortunately, was not enough. The door remained closed.

"Too bad we can't tell him that perhaps as soon as tomorrow he can go out," Nick's father said. Bending down, he petted the cat. At this, Horace gave out a low baritone miaow and his black tail twitched. "Anyhow, he was out for a little while."

"Long enough to chase a spiddle," Nick said.

"Think of the joy he'll feel," his father said, "when he runs and frisks. When he shouts to the sky the greatness of his bold spirit. That fine, free spirit will be released from what, for him, must be captivity. Poor old Horace." Nick's father continued to pet Horace. Horace continued to try to induce him, by many a dulcet sound and many an intense look, to open the door.

"Tomorrow," Nick told the cat.

"A new universe awaits him," Nick's father said. "No wonder he's impatient. It awaits us, too. Once we destroy that plant, that—" He broke off, his face somber.

"The Grand Four are on our side," Nick pointed out. "So we're not alone." Thank heaven for that, he thought to himself.

"I wish we still had that book," Nick's mother said. "If only we could have at least read it."

"Maybe we can get it back," Nick said. But, at the moment, he had no idea how.

Chapter 10

THE next morning, after a moderately sufferable sleep, Nick awoke, dressed, and, with his mother and father, had breakfast in the kitchen at the little table which had been there when they arrived. Horace worried away at a dish of synthetic shrimp-pellets, this, too, having been supplied by the government.

A knock sounded on the front door.

"I'll get it," Nick's father said. He rose from the table, walked to the living room and peered out through the window. "People," he said. "Possibly neighbors." He unlocked and opened the front door.

A man, short and round and almost bald, stood on the porch. With him a thin woman, her hair tied up in a black net, stood fussily waiting. "I'm Jack McKenna," the man said to Nick's father. "And this is my wife, Doris. We're from down the road. We saw you move in last night, and we would have come and helped you…except that at night the trobes and the werjes roam this world, looking for stray colonists so unwise as to venture out after dark."

Mrs. McKenna said, "We saw a police hovercar come to your place last night. What happened?" Her eyes were big with curiosity.

"A father-thing," Nick's dad said. "Growing by the house. Come in." He ushered the McKennas into the living room. "We're just finishing breakfast. Would you like a cup of coffee?"

"Please join us," Nick's mother said. "I'm Helen Graham; this is my husband, Pete." She nodded towards Nick. "And our boy. Nicholas."

"You have a cat," Mrs. McKenna said, noticing Horace. "He won't last long, here. A werj will fly off with him."

"The werjes already flew off with Horace," Nick said. "But they gave him back."

"Strange," Mr. McKenna said, his brow wrinkling. "Werjes very rarely do that. I wonder why."

Nick's mother served coffee to the McKennas, who seemed glad to be offered it; they seated themselves in the living room, across from Nick's father, and sipped from their plastic cups.

"You realize, don't you," Mr. McKenna said presently, "that the native life forms here on Plowman's Planet are locked in a death struggle which has been going on for centuries?"

"Yes," Nick's father said, nodding. "We're aware of it. The werjes told us."

"Most of the human colonists who have come here," Mrs. McKenna said, "would like to go elsewhere, because of this war. Even back to Earth, as overcrowded as it is."

"We can't go back," Nick said. "Because of Horace."

"Is a cat a big enough reason to become castaways from your own world?" Mrs. McKenna asked, in a haughty voice.

Nick's father said quietly. "It's a matter of principle. We feel there should be room enough for animals, no matter how crowded the planet gets."

"You're going to farm, here?" Mr. McKenna asked. "You're going to plough the land and plant a crop?"

"Exactly," Nick's father said, nodding.

"Any experience doing that?" Mrs. McKenna asked.

"Not yet," Nick's father admitted. "But I've brought books along with me, about farming. I intend to read up on it."

"You won't be able to make a go of it," Mrs. McKenna said in a gloomy voice.

"I think Pete will," Nick's mother said. "He's always been a determined and original man. And a man who lives out his convictions to the fullest."

An evil, long face appeared at the living room window. Its eyes gleamed: tiny slits like aged celluloid. Nick realized it was wearing a pair of dark glasses.

"Good lord!" Nick's father said, leaping up. "What's *that*?"

"A trobe," Mr. McKenna said calmly. "They know you're here and they want to get a look at you. The werjes probably told them."

"Isn't there anything we can do?" Nick's mother asked nervously. "Is it dangerous?"

"You can drive it off with this," Mr. McKenna said; he handed Nick's father a small metal device which had hung from his belt. "A trobe-beam. It emits a bright light, and trobes faint in the presence of extreme light, despite their dark glasses. Just show it the trobe-beam and it'll probably go."

The trobe, however, had already disappeared. Perhaps it had seen the trobe-beam which Mr. McKenna carried.

"A trobe," Mr. McKenna said, "will pelt you with rocks; that is a trobe's contribution to the war. They are not nearly as harmful as the werjes, and neither werjes nor trobes are as bad as the father-things. But of all of them, father-things, werjes, trobes—Glimmung is the most dangerous and the one to be avoided."

"I saw him," Nick said.

"Where?" both Mr. and Mrs. McKenna asked, instantly.

"Inside a werj," Nick said.

"So that's where Glimmung has gone, these days," Mr. McKenna said, nodding. "I'm not surprised. That way he can direct the werjes so that they can carry off more nunks and spiddles, and possibly a few human colonists. Although humans are a little too heavy for one werj to handle. And we are all armed against werjes."

"In what way?" asked Nick's father.

Mr. McKenna said, "Werjes fear strong, strange smells. In particular, the smell of things not natural to this planet. All of us carry an onion around with us, or perhaps a dead frog or other minor creature from Earth. You would do well to do so, too."

"What about garlic?" Nick's mother asked.

"For some reason, werjes like the smell of garlic," Mr. McKenna answered. "I suggest you try a rose, if you have one. Or a bit of lavender. Or—"

"Wisteria," Mrs. McKenna interrupted. "Werjes are terrified of the smell of wisteria. And of carnations. But carnations won't grow here on Plowman's Planet. Unfortunately."

Nick's mother said haltingly, "I have a little bottle of perfume."

"That would undoubtedly do it," Mrs. McKenna said.

Once more the trobe came to the window, or perhaps it was another trobe entirely. Nick could not tell. The trobe peered in, its yellow, tiny face alive with a wild, warped hate. It rapped on the glass with a hairy, skinny knuckle. And spoke.

"What's it saying?" Nick's father demanded.

"The cat," Mr. McKenna said. "Something about your cat."

The trobe pressed its rubbery lips to the window and repeated what it had said.

"Good lord," Nick's father said, leaping up. "It's saying they've got Horace." He looked around quickly. "But Horace is in here!"

"The front door," Nick's mother said faintly. "It's open a crack. He must have got out."

"Sorry," Mr. McKenna said, but he did not seem very concerned. "I guess I forgot to close it. Or maybe it doesn't fit quite right. A lot of these government-built houses aren't much good."

At the window, the trobe called, "...eat him ...best dinner in months..." The trobe then disappeared from sight. It had gone.

Nick said huskily, "They're going to eat Horace." He ran to the front door and out on to the porch.

"Nick, come back!" his father called from behind him. "The Nick-thing—we have to look for it first!"

But Nick had already seen two trobes making off with Horace; a trobe holding each end. The trobes were not large, but between them they managed to carry the cat, despite Horace's vigorous kicking and twisting.

"Let go of my cat!" Nick yelled. And he started after them.

Chapter 11

As Nick ran after the trobes, something stirred in the orange shrubbery which grew on both sides of the road.

"Hey, mister," a voice called. It was a spiddle, standing erect among the bushes, trying to attract Nick's attention.

"They've got my cat," Nick panted, halting. "They're going to eat him." He started blindly on.

"Wait, wait," the spiddle said, gesturing. Another spiddle appeared and then two more. A whole group of spiddles now poked their noses up on both sides of the road, all of them trying to talk at once. "Hold it," the first spiddle said loudly, waving for silence. "Come on, fellas," the spiddle said, with irritation. "Okay, all ready."

"I can't listen," Nick said.

"Mister, it's a trap," the first spiddle said. "They're not going to eat that nut-head animal of yours; they're just trying to lure you out of the house."

"Why?" Nick said. But he waited to hear. Far down the road

the two trobes, wearing their dark glasses, lugging Horace, trotted; he watched them grow smaller.

"We understand there's a Nick-thing in action," the first spiddle said. "We've been looking for it all night, but no luck. It's *you* that's going to get eaten, if you're not more careful. This is danger city, out here, as long as that thing is wandering around."

Nick broke free from his indecision. He ran on down the road, in the direction which the trobes had taken.

The road led into a vast mass of trees, a lightless place of deep shadow and vines.

"Stay out of there!" the spiddles called after him. Some of them appeared on the road, as if to follow him.

Nick entered the dark grove.

To the right, just off the road, he saw something which he had not expected to see. Shocked, he stood still, staring. The ancient car, Reg Frankis' water tank. The car had turned over. The water tank, split in half, still leaked out steady streams of liquid; a pool had formed around the car and the broken tank.

Not far off, amid the twisted bushes, lay the water man, face-down. A shaft of silvery metal projected upwards from the centre of his back. The water man, Reg Frankis, was dead.

A spiddle, coming up beside Nick, said, "Glimmung's spear."

"In the middle of his back," Nick said thickly.

"Thus does Glimmung operate," the spiddle said.

The car had been torn open. Parts of it were strewn everywhere, as if a giant had rooted in it, seeking something.

"Looking for the book," the spiddle said. "The world-book, the book which changes every time it's read. The book which is never the same. The only copy, which you gave to the water man."

"It's my fault," Nick said. "If I hadn't traded it to him—"

"Then Glimmung would have done you in," the spiddle said. "He would do anything to get his book back. Cowardly assault city. Just as we would do anything to get it for ourselves." The spiddle was silent a moment, thinking. "This is a stunted spot, here in this grove; everything here is misshapen. Forget your animal, mister. Go back to your house. The trobes have lured you here to destroy you. This place is destruction city."

Nick said, "I'm staying here." He had an idea which he did not wish to share with the spiddle. "Go back to my house," he said, "and tell my father what's happened. I'll meet him here."

"Stay on the road, then," the spiddle said, It started back in the direction which the two of them had come. "Don't let them coax you off the road, as they did the water man." The spiddle waited a moment, then hurried off once more. In a moment it was gone.

Nick thought, *The book may still be here.*

Where, he asked himself, would the water man hide it? In a car, a driver would put something the size of a book, something small, into the glove compartment. Yes, he remembered the water man doing that. And werjes—and perhaps also Glimmung—would not know that. They would not know, in fact, what a glove compartment was, or where it could be found.

Opening the bent, broken door of the car, Nick slid carefully inside. His groping fingers touched the button of the glove compartment and he pressed. The door of the glove compartment did not open. He pressed the button again. Still it did not open.

It's jammed, Nick said to himself. I'll have to pry it open.

Getting back out of the car he searched about, among the strewn wreckage, until he found a sharp triangle of metal. This will do it, he decided; once more he crawled gingerly into the car, and this time he wedged the piece of metal into the slot around the door of the glove compartment.

The little door fell open. Nick peered in.

Lying within, the book. Glimmung's book.

Nick lifted it out and crawled back out of the car; he stood in the half-darkness of the trees, reading its cover. *One Summer Day,* the book he had traded with the water man; the book which the werj, by mistake, had given him.

Should I tell anyone? he asked himself. I guess not, he decided. They would think it was too dangerous.

Nick unbuttoned his shirt and put the small, dry book inside it, then buttoned his shirt back up. No one will know, he said to himself.

From a nearby tree, something flapped. A shape ascended into the morning sky—Nick turned in fear to watch it go. A werj. It had been resting among the branches.

Did it see me? Nick asked himself. Did it see the book? He did not know. Time would tell.

The werj flew soundlessly away, in the direction of a distant line of worn, tattered mountains. Nick watched until the werj disappeared from sight. He thought, Maybe it's gone to tell Glimmung.

"Nick!" His father and Mr. McKenna came hurrying along the road from the house; ahead of them a spiddle leaped and raced, like a many-tailed squirrel. Behind his father other spiddles hurried, too.

"I'm fine," Nick said, as his father and Mr. McKenna entered the gloomy grove of trees.

"You shouldn't have left the house," his father said, pale with alarm. "Any sign of—" He saw, then, what had happened to the water man.

"Glimmung," Nick said, in explanation.

"I'll call the police," Mr. McKenna said. He glanced in fear up into the trees. "It's isn't safe to be here, for any of us. Glimmung must be very angry; this doesn't often happen, an outright act like this, especially against humans. Usually they're more interested in the printers." Mr. McKenna started back towards the house, leaving Nick and his father and the spiddles.

"No sign of Horace?" Nick's father asked.

Nick said, "The two trobes went in here; I saw them go in, but then I saw Mr. Frankis. And I stopped following them."

"I guess we've lost Horace," his father said gently.

"Maybe so," Nick said. But he didn't believe it. "The spiddles said—" he started to say, but his father interrupted him.

"Nick, I'm taking you back to the house. We'll wait for the police there." His hand firmly on Nick's shoulder, he led him back up the road, in the direction from which they had come.

One of the spiddles was speaking excitedly to another. "Hey, George—maybe the book is still here. Let's take a look." Both spiddles, and then a third, crept into the wrecked car and began to fuss about inside.

"Come on," Nick's father said, and urged his son along. "Think what it'll mean to the last surviving printers," one of the spiddles chattered eagerly. "If we can only find it, finally."

To his father, Nick said, "About the book—"

"Forget the book," his father said. "It's not important."

Oh yes it is, Nick said to himself.

Chapter 12

Back in the house, Nick shut himself up in his room. There, in privacy, he unbuttoned his shirt and got out the book. Seating himself, he opened to the index in the back part and looked under the name *Frankis, Reg.* What was it the spiddles had said? "The world-book. The book which changes every time it's read." And the spiddles, before that, had said something else. "It's all there. Everything—the past and the future. Both."

Under *Frankis, Reg* the index gave a page number. Page 42. Nick turned to that page, and, his fingers shaking as he held the book, read the text. He read:

"'...for his thieving ways. Alas, alas, but Glimmung knew that it had to be done. The water man had no right to the book. And so he vanished. And his water tank—smashed forever. *Pax vobiscum.*'"

Yes, there it was. Right in the book. A short but accurate account of Mr. Frankis' death. Had this passage been here yesterday? Nick wondered. Suppose he had looked this up, on the car trip to the house? Suppose Mr. Frankis had looked for his own name in the index? Would he have found this—and known what was going to happen to him?

But the spiddles had said, "The book which changes every time it's read." So maybe this passage had not been here, before now. It had appeared at the time of Mr. Frankis' death, or else after.

What is there in the book about me? Nick wondered. The text which we read before, on the way here, after Glimmung accidentally gave the book to me? Or by now has it changed?

Again Nick looked in the index, this time under *Graham, Peter & family*. The index gave page 5, this time. Hadn't it given page 31 before? Nick asked himself. I'm sure that's what it said, then, he thought.

He turned to page 5. And read:

"'The boy will receive a book by mistake. A valuable book. He will trade it and lose it, and then regain it. Trobes, two of them, will carry off the creature who smells of fish. But that creature will bite them and free himself. The creature will wander in the forests of the world. He will cry by day and by night. The boy will find him by his cries. But Glimmung will learn who has his book, and he will come seeking the boy.'"

That ended the passage about Nick.

Nick thought, It wasn't there before. The spiddles are right; the book changes.

And the book knows the future; it knows that Horace will bite the trobes and escape. And that I'll find him again, by means of his yowls.

That was one sure thing about Horace: he had an overly large yowl, which he used when necessary, and sometimes when it was not.

What does it have to say in the index under *Horace*? Nick wondered. Again he turned to the index. Yes, there was an entry for Horace. On page 8, the index said; there he would find an entry about the cat.

He turned to page 8. And read:

"'The creature who smells of fish will find his way, one day, to the ocean. Then he will be grey and very old. He will go down to the ocean and he will make a certain cry. At that cry, a great fish will come, which will open its mouth, and into the great fish the creature will go. The fish will carry him out to sea, and there will be crying and the chant of sorrowful people.'"

Nick wondered how far in the future that would happen, when Horace would find his way to the ocean and the great fish. But—at least Horace would get away from the two trobes. And he himself would find the cat.

That meant the Glimmung would not get in and destroy him, at least not for a while.

If Glimmung comes, Nick decided, I'll hand the book over to him. That would be wise, in view of what he can do. But—

If only, Nick thought, I had time to make a copy of the book. It would take hours to do, perhaps even days. And what he copied would not change, as did the book itself.

And then it came to him, the realisation of what he must do. If I can find a printer, he said to himself, it could make a duplicate of the book. An exact copy. If, he thought, I'm right as to what printers do. I can ask the spiddles; they'll know.

Going from his room, he made his way to the front door, opened it, and looked out into the shrubbery of the yard. His father and mother and Mr. McKenna were nowhere in sight; evidently they must have gone back to the grove of trees, where Mr. Frankis was, to wait for the police to come.

"Calling all spiddles," Nick said loudly. "Come in, spiddles. Do you hear me?"

A sleepy spiddle-head popped up; the spiddle had obviously been taking a nap. "Interruption city," the spiddle said, and shook his head to clear it. "What's the action, mister?" he asked Nick.

Nick said, "Can you take me to a printer?"

"The other mister, the bigger mister, said you should stay inside," the spiddle pointed out. "I heard him. Incarceration city; that's what it is" The spiddle eased himself back down into the shrubbery once more, to resume his nap.

Taking a deep breath, Nick said, "I have Glimmung's book again."

At once, four spiddle-heads popped up; the four spiddles stared at him: eight unwinking eyes that shone like morning dew.

"You're putting us on," one of the spiddles said. "I'll lay it in front," it said to its companions. "He doesn't have Glimmung's book. Glimmung got it back from the water man. We ourselves looked all around."

Nick said, "I had the book before you began to look."

"Revelation city," a spiddle said, an awed, hopeful expression on its gnarled little brown face. "What are you going to do with it, mister? We don't have any money; neither do the printers. Maybe some other human colonists have."

"It isn't a question of money," Nick said. "It's a question of me saving myself from what happened to Mr. Frankis."

"Then give us the book," a spiddle suggested.

Nick said, "Glimmung would still think I had it. He'll go on thinking this until I give it back to him." But, secretly, Nick had another reason for keeping the book. He wanted to read it, and not just now but always; he wanted the book to remain his forever.

The spiddles seemed to guess this, because one of them said, "I think you're being foolish, mister, to hang on to Glimmung's book. You'd be a lot safer if you gave it to us. But we understand. A book like that, a book which can do what it does, is hard to forget about. All right; we'll settle for a copy; we'll take you to the nearest of the printers and get it to make a replica of Glimmung's book...which it will be most glad to do. We have been searching for this book, praying Glimmung would lose it, for years. Opportunity city. Come on." The spiddles leaped from the shrubbery and scooted down the path, looking back to be sure that Nick was following.

High above them, in the sky, a black dot circled.

"A werj," the spiddles murmured as they led Nick on to the road.

"Can it see us from that far away?" Nick asked uneasily.

"Probably," a spiddle said. "Do you have anything on you which would discourage a werj? Some odor-producing object, such as an onion?"

"No," Nick said. "I forgot to get an onion. I meant to, but—"

"Here's a valuable, anti-werj item that a human colonist gave me," one of the spiddles said; evidently the hope of getting hold of

Glimmung's book at last had made the spiddles reckless. "A piece of blue cheese," the spiddle said, as Nick reached out his hand.

"A werj would die," another spiddle added, "if it got within ten yards of this strange blue cheese object. What is it used for, on your home planet?"

Nick said, "Blue cheese is eaten there."

"Incredibility city," the spiddles said in unison. They hopped rapidly on, with Nick keeping up with them. The journey to the printer had begun, despite the werj hanging far above them in the mid-morning sky. Glancing up, a spiddle said, "I hope it can't tell what we're doing."

I'm taking what my dad would call a "calculated risk", Nick said to himself. He'll be very angry when he finds me gone, angry and worried. But—this is the only way I can rid myself of Glimmung's attention, at least, Nick pondered, without giving up the book.

Which, he thought, I do not intend to do.

Chapter 13

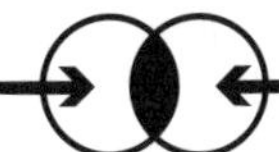

How far," Nick asked, after an interval of walking, "is the printer? Will it take us much longer?"

"Not far," a spiddle said, puffing for breath.

Above them, the werj had been joined by a second black dot. Two werjes now circled, keeping directly above them, and yet doing nothing. Nick thought, They must not be able to see the book; they must not know that I have it.

He had once again buttoned up his shirt over the book. Against his skin the book felt as dry and scratchy as the pelt of a wild, unnatural serpent. As before, he did not enjoy the feel of it.

"Where did the trobes get the dark glasses they wear?" Nick asked the spiddles.

"Originally, years ago, they stole one pair from a colonist," the spiddles answered. "And then they forced a printer, whom they had caught, to make many, many copies for them."

Nick asked, "Do you have a trobe-beam with you? To shine at them if they attack?"

"Yep," the spiddles said. "Protection city," one added, with glee. The spiddles did not seem to feel the fear of trobes that they felt towards Glimmung and the werjes.

"Did the printer get away again?" Nick asked.

A spiddle said, "Unfortunately no. Finally Glimmung stuck it with his spear. Anyhow, that printer had become very old and frail. That is why the trobes could take it captive. Disparity city."

"What does 'disparity' mean?" Nick asked.

"Well," a spiddle began. And then all the spiddles fell to arguing about it; they chattered like angry mice.

"Let it go," Nick said.

"Incomprehensibility city," one of the spiddles said, concluding the argument.

The orange bushes and grass on both sides of the road had begun to give way to pale desert, a dry stretch where nothing grew. No place for us to hide if we're attacked, Nick realized. But, at the same time, no place for trobes to ambush us. He could see for miles, now, as could the spiddles.

Something small and round rolled across the road ahead of them. Something alive.

"A nunk," the spiddles told him. "This is a place of nunks, here, where nothing grows. The war has forced the once prosperous nunks to take up residence in certain barren surroundings."

"Hello, there!" the nunk called in a squeaky, small voice.

"How do, nunk," the spiddles answered; they did not slow down, and neither did Nick.

"Where you going so fast?" the nunk inquired. It rolled back on to the road; Nick had to be careful not to step on it.

"A printer," the spiddles declared. "We're looking for old Lord Blue. Or has he expired?"

The nunk said cheerfully, "Lord Blue is busy as usual turning out toasters and waffle irons and radios for the colonists. Who's this young colonist, here? We haven't seen him before."

"My family and I just arrived from Earth," Nick said. And then he thought, Was it only *yesterday* that we came here? So much has happened…and in less than one full day.

"Bit of warning," the nunk said as it rolled along with them. "You see the werjes up above? I've been listening to their talk. They think that this young colonist knows where Glimmung's book is. What say you to that, young colonist? Any retort on your part?"

Nick said cautiously, "I gave it to the water man."

"The werjes say they didn't find it," the nunk said, zipping about between their feet, as if it were a game. "They looked and then they gave up; they decided that the water man never had it."

"That's not so," Nick said.

"Another thing," the nunk said. "A father-thing is following after you."

Chilled, Nick said, "One that looks like me?"

"Exactly like you," the nunk said, and then happily rolled away, leaving Nick and the spiddles.

"That's not good news," a spiddle said presently.

"We better not slow down," another said. "Urgency city; let's hurry."

Nick and the spiddles hurried.

Above them, the werjes continued to circle.

Chapter 14

THE desert became a rising slope on which odd spike-like plants grew, shafts of mottled grey on which no leaves could be seen. The plants, to Nick, seemed old and dead. They did not stir in the faint midday wind. It was like an orchard which had been abandoned. On some of the plants little dried fruits hung, withered and stale. And, off along a cracked, desolate side road, what appeared to be the ruins of a farmhouse could be made out. Someone, Nick decided, lived here, once. Perhaps a human being. But that person had given up, had gone away. Never to return.

"Once this was a ripe, rich field, a place of many harvests," a spiddle said in a somber voice. "Then Glimmung came. He blasted this region with his presence; he made the settlers go away. That was years back."

"I see," Nick said, and shivered.

"Glimmung took all the life here away," the spiddle went on.

"He drained it from the ground; he stole it from the plants. The man and woman who tilled and farmed here became stiff and brittle, like parched bone. Because of that they couldn't stay. Others have tried to come here, since then, but it's always the same; they always leave. Glimmung's curse hangs over this land, and always will. At least until Glimmung himself is destroyed."

"Which probably will never happen," another spiddle

"Maybe it will," Nick said.

"If it happens," one of the spiddles said, "it will not be our doing. Spiddles can't really accomplish very much. Impotence city, I'd say."

Ahead, low hills confronted them, bleak and evidently uninhabited. Nick saw huge boulders of some kind of white rock; the color did not please him, nor did it seem to make the spiddles very happy either. In silence, he and the spiddles ascended a rough and twisting trail which passed between heaps of once-molten slag. As if, Nick thought, a dead volcano exists here, nearby. Its fire gone, perhaps for many decades, perhaps for as much as a thousand years.

Ahead, on the ragged peak of a hill, Nick saw a wide irregular cleft, as if lightning had hurled itself down, burning this awesome slot into the dim, cold rise of earth.

"Glimmung's mark," a spiddle said. All the spiddles paused in their climb and so did Nick. "At that spot, over there, Glimmung first appeared on this world. He flashed down out of the midday sky, shedding grey fire, burning everything he came near. Since then nothing has lived here. Out of this place, Glimmung spread over all the planet, like a lake of hateful night. Fire and night; that is Glimmung's way. That is his nature."

The spiddles, having rested, started on once more.

"Is it far, now?" Nick asked, panting as he ascended step by step.

"On the plain beyond these hills," the spiddles gasped; they, also, were nearly spent. Weight hung on them, a burden conferred by this place. Even to walk here took enormous strength; Nick felt as if the world itself had settled on to his back, bowing him and bending him. He felt weary and very old, as if he had lived for a thousand years.

"Fatigue," a spiddle panted, "is everywhere, here. As if gravity forages from these hills, searching for living things to infest with its weight. But it won't be long, now."

Above them, the two werjes had been joined by a third. And now a fourth werj flap-flapped towards the others, to take up its station with them.

"They must know where we're going," Nick said.

"True," a spiddle agreed. "But werjes are afraid of printers. Printers have a power over other creatures…at least when the printer is strong. But they are so weakened, now. The struggle with Glimmung has gone on so long."

They had reached the top; here, they paused. Nick looked down the far side of the hill and saw, below, level land stretching out, with grass and an occasional tree. And, here and there, a farmhouse. Human colonists evidently lived here, a fair number of them, in fact.

"Now the journey will be easier," a spiddle told him; the spiddle got out a large handkerchief and noisily blew its nose. Another spiddle dabbed delicately at its forehead, where perspiration shone.

"Exhaustion city," a spiddle commented.

For a short while longer they paused, here at the crest of the range of hills. And then, one by one, they started down the far side.

Above, the four werjes suddenly dropped, their wings folded. They descended directly towards Nick and the group of spiddles.

"Quick!" a spiddle shouted. "The blue cheese!"

Nick took the cheese out of his pocket and held it towards the descending werjes. In a frenzy of revulsion, the four werjes swept in a long glide, away from the spiddles and Nick; the werjes shrieked in disgust, hovered for a moment and then streaked off, in the direction from which Nick and the spiddles had come.

"They were only trying to frighten us," a spiddle said. But all the spiddles looked frightened.

"Keep the blue cheese ready," a spiddle said to Nick, who still held the werj repellent. "They may sneak back behind us, to seize us when we are not looking. Once we are with Lord Blue," the spiddle continued, "it will be all right."

Again they descended the broken path, step by step. Now tall weeds grew, harsh and mean; the weeds showed spines like stings, and the spiddles carefully avoided them. Evidently the stings were poisonous. But at last the evil weeds thinned out, and harmless orange grass replaced them. The spiddles relaxed, now, and chattered amiably among themselves. It appeared to Nick that, for a time, the danger had ended.

"There is the printer," a spiddle said, halting for a moment to point. Nick shaded his eyes and peered.

Below them a group of human colonists clustered around a shapeless cone which radiated wet, dull colors, a mound of immense size which pulsed, ebbed and flowed and then reformed itself.

"Is that it?" Nick said, disappointed.

"Don't let the printer's physical form discourage you," one of the spiddles said. "It is, admittedly, rather plain. But a printer is intelligent and kind, full of wise goodwill and the determination to help all who come to it. Assistance city; that's what a printer is." The spiddle began to move on, and the others joined it. Nick did, too.

When they reached the level ground, Nick saw that the human colonists surrounding the printer carried all sorts of appliances which they wanted copied. One by one, the colonists brought precious possessions up to Lord Blue, and, undulating with effort, the great old printer produced, from itself, a reproduction of the object. At first the reproductions looked identical to the original objects to Nick, but as he got closer he saw that, in every case, the printer's reproduction was inferior. Seeing this, he remembered all that he had heard about the printers: their weariness, their age, their inability to keep their reproductions from becoming—what was the word? Puddinged; that was it. A good term, Nick decided as he viewed that which the printer had made.

The printer's products were indistinct and vaguely-defined. Nick saw, over to one side, a colonist who had got the printer to duplicate a pocket watch for him; going that way, Nick caught a glimpse of the face of the watch. All the numbers were there, but in the wrong order. The six, he saw, was at the top, and the twelve where the four should have been. And—the watch had no hands.

Feeling keen disappointment, Nick moved in the direction of a colonist who held a bowl which the printer had made. The bowl, as Nick watched, came apart. Pieces of it fell as the bowl shattered. The man looked unhappy, but not surprised. They must be used to this, Nick realized. And yet they keep coming here. But then he thought, So do I. I guess, he thought, they keep hoping.

Going up the path to the printer, Nick waited while a woman ahead of him carefully set down a white and black ivory chess set which she wanted duplicated.

The printer surged and trembled, and then a portion of him came loose, forming a separate, small mound. The mound settled, gained color; it became black at one end, white at the other. The mound then divided into smaller pieces, and these solidified into black and white chessmen. But—

"Oh dear," the woman said in dismay. "I'm afraid you don't have it right, Lord Blue. There should be only two kings and two queens; the pieces should be different." She showed the printer the original set. "Don't you see?" she asked.

Nick moved closer to see. Yes, the various chessmen were all the same. Each had assumed a mere upright shape, without features; it was not possible to tell them apart. And, even as he watched, the pieces sagged, as if melting. They dwindled into puddles of black and white which then blended together into a neutral grey. It was no longer possible even to tell that it was intended to be a chess set.

"Won't you try again?" the woman asked. "You used to be able to do so much better; even last month, in fact."

A uniformed man, standing near the printer, said to her, "One try only is allowed. Step aside for the next person, ma'am. Lord

Blue is very weak, today. You." The uniformed man beckoned to Nick. "Your turn," he said to Nick. "And don't strain him too much," he added.

Nick began unbuttoning his shirt. He took hold of the book and lifted it out.

"Glimmung's book!" the woman behind Nick cried.

The uniformed man stared at the book, then at Nick. His face showed fear, much to Nick's surprise. All the people, on every side of Nick, retreated in panic. Are they that much afraid of Glimmung? Nick asked himself. He, himself, felt far more uneasy, now; their fear told him much. "I want to have a duplicate made of it," Nick said. "Then we can return the original to Glimmung. And keep the copy."

At his feet, spiddles squirmed and yammered; Nick could not make out what they were saying. And then he saw the people looking up; he saw their stricken, frozen faces as they saw something above and towards the hills from which Nick and the spiddles had come.

"It is Glimmung," the spiddles said in hushed voices. "He is coming here; he has seen the book."

In the sky the shape of Glimmung grew larger and larger.

Chapter 15

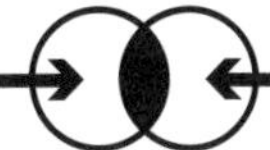

GLIMMUNG had ceased to hide within the werj. Now, in a form of his own, he swept like a visible wind towards Nick, straining to hurry. Glimmung came as fast as he could, called forth by the book, his book, the book from which he ruled this world.

He had a broken quality, as if his body had been fractured into many sections and then incorrectly, inexpertly repaired. No puddinged product by an aging printer could match his inexactness; the fraudulent circumference of his lame, malformed trunk; his twisted, beckoning eyes. Glimmung called as he descended, a whine that made Nick's ears shudder: a noise which sent the spiddles rushing aimlessly, unable to stand it even for a moment. Glimmung was speaking, but Nick could not make out the words; the creature's speech blurred together, like a record gone wrong.

How large he is, Nick thought as he stood watching. And still Glimmung was yet a long distance off; he grew as he fell from the sky. Still he expanded, and in his eyes a massive cold cruelty gleamed, eyes like deranged stars. Eyes, Nick thought, that picked out the thread of evil everywhere, knitting the thread into a fabric which Glimmung meant as a cover for the world.

Delight showed on Glimmung's mocking, shining face; delight at seeing his book once more—a frigid, shrieking joy at being close to the all-knowing book again. Glimmung loved the book; he could not live apart from it. Without it he waned; he became hollow. With the book, Glimmung's power returned. Descending from the sky, Glimmung reached to grasp it; he extended himself avidly, and his whining voice became a furious song, a song of triumph and possession. It is my book, the song declared. It was lost by mistake; now it has been returned.

Nick tucked the book back in to his shirt; again he clasped it against his chest, and felt its leathery presence next to him. He ran. And in the sky, Glimmung altered his course; he held out his right arm, and in his hand Nick saw a spear, the spear of Glimmung which had killed the water man Mr. Frankis and many other innocent creatures besides.

"Give *me* the book!" Glimmung wailed, and his voice danced in the wind, the wind created by his own enormous descent.

"Give him the book," the spiddles chattered to Nick in fright; they milled everywhere, not leaving him, as had the human colonists. "He will kill you," the spiddles whimpered. "And us along with you. There's no hope; this is surrender city. Let him have it back."

What can I do? Nick asked himself. Can the printer help me? Still a round, inert mass, the printer remained unstirring; there was nothing the printer could do. Or, Nick thought, nothing it could think of; it had become too old to think. Where can I get help? Nick asked himself. My father is a long way from here; Horace is wandering in the forests, after biting the trobes. There is only myself, here with this book, with Glimmung's book. And now he will get it back. And the war, Nick thought; it will go on, and perhaps Glimmung will win. He will use his book as before, and nothing will stand against him; he will be too strong. But, he thought, the book; could it help me?

Crouching, Nick groped within his shirt. The book tumbled out and he snatched it up; he turned to the back, to the index. He looked under 'G', under *Glimmung*. Many pages about Glimmung; many entries and sections. How Glimmung came; what Glimmung had done; what Glimmung planned. And—one final entry.

How Glimmung could be destroyed.

Page 45, the index said. The final page in the book. Nick turned to page 45, and, as above his head Glimmung wheeled and screamed and reached to grasp his book, Nick scanned the text.

"'...and he can be destroyed by nothing; he will never end. He will outlast them all. But he can he weakened, so much so that he will not recover; he can be made powerless and small, for all the time that is to come.'"

Nick shouted, "How?"

The text continued, "'Place the book before the printer so that Glimmung is lured close; so that he must, in order to snatch the book, come against the printer and within the printer's range. If this is done—'" But at that moment Nick felt the frigid breath of Glimmung close on his neck. Shutting the book, Nick ran back towards the printer. Over his head Glimmung wheeled, and then, like thunder, the spear unleashed itself; the spear hurled into the ground by Nick, its shaft whipping and vibrating. Glimmung, overhead, cursed to see it miss; he dropped and reached for it, descending almost to the ground.

Nick placed the book against the soft, high side of the printer. And then ran back, out of the way.

Seeing the book, Glimmung forgot his spear; he came to rest, his cape curling about him like a tongue of jagged, ominous flame. He strode to the printer, huge in his contempt; there, beside the printer, he bent down and with powerful fingers picked up the book. He remained there, holding the book, looking at Nick with hatred.

The printer shuddered and rose up high. It formed itself into a column and from that column there sprang a phantom Glimmung. The printer, in its death agony, had duplicated Glimmung, a poor duplicate, to be sure, but nonetheless alive and great of size. The duplicate Glimmung, his horned helmet glistening, his eyes hot with malice, raised his phantom spear and plunged it into the throat of Glimmung himself.

Glimmung rushed upward, into the sky, the book clasped in one gloved hand. From him the spear protruded, and as he climbed he reached at it; he tried to tug it from him. The spear remained, and from it there appeared a wound which did not close; Glimmung could not remove the spear and he could not heal the wound. He had been pierced, and he would carry with him the injury which the inexact, ill-formed duplicate Glimmung had given him—would carry it through eternity.

On the ground the phantom Glimmung turned to face Nick; it raised its gloved hands beseechingly, and then fell back into itself. It collapsed into formlessness into a puddinged mass with neither contour nor shape. It fell to the earth and lay still, and as it lay it lost motion and the imitation life which had animated it; dying, the phantom Glimmung joined the dying printer which had fashioned it.

"Glimmung is hurt!" the spiddles cried, gathering around Nick, trying to help him up—the force of Glimmung's gaze had thrown him to his hands and knees. "He is gone; he fled. He is maimed forever. He came too close to the printer; in his eagerness to get back his book he strayed too far—he forgot his enemy."

"Salvation city!" another group of spiddles, hurrying from beyond the printer, declared.

Nick said huskily, "He got the book back."

"But he will never be the same," a spiddle said. "The spear in his throat will leech his life; he will not be the same as before. Get up, mister, before the werjes come. Glimmung may strike in revenge by means of them. Remember your piece of blue cheese," the spiddle went on. "It will protect you from Glimmung's wrath."

"Glimmung's wrath," the other spiddles chanted. "You must be kept safe; you have won a victory for us. You have saved us all."

"Not quite," Nick said with difficulty; he stood swaying, finding himself weak and confused. His vision blurred and he shook his head, trying to clear it and to steady himself. To the spiddles he said, "I can't make it home. One of you go get my father and ask him to come here. Will I be safe here for a while?"

The uniformed colonist, who had stood guard beside the printer, came rapidly up to Nick; he steadied him with his hand, saying, "You'll be absolutely all right here. We have werj-repellants and trobe-beams, and Glimmung himself won't be back for some time. Maybe never. He may retreat to his mountains and hide himself there, waiting to become healed. But nothing that is stabbed through by Glimmung's spear can heal itself; he'll wait there in the mountains, in his high places, forever."

"Is there any place I can sit down?" Nick asked.

A colonist hurried up with the duplicate of a chair which the printer had, a little while ago, made. "Sit on this," he said to Nick. He and the uniformed man helped Nick seat himself on the chair.

The legs of the chair were various lengths; under Nick the chair teetered and sank on one side, so that once more he had to stand. The printer had not done a very good job.

"I'm okay now," Nick said. "More or less." He examined his shirt and found it covered with countless tiny crystals of ice which had rained on to him from Glimmung's great dark cape. "All I have to do now," Nick said aloud, "is find Horace." In all this, he had not for one minute forgotten his cat.

He would not be happy again, despite his victory over Glimmung, until Horace was found.

Chapter 16

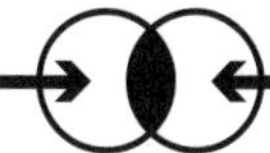

WHAT had Glimmung's book said about Horace? He would thrash about and bite the trobes, it had said. He would escape, and Nick would hear his cries as Horace roamed the forests of Plowman's Planet. So I must listen for him, Nick realized. I must find him by the loud sounds he will make…is perhaps already making now.

His father had at last come, and with him Mr. McKenna. Apparently Mrs. McKenna and his mother were waiting back at the house.

"You never should have gone outside again," his father said to him reprovingly; he seemed very worried and tense, as much so as he had been back on Earth. "It's just luck that they didn't get you, those flying werjes or whatever they're called."

"Not luck," Nick corrected. He showed his father the blue cheese. "This protects me," he said. "Ask Mr. McKenna."

Mr. McKenna agreed. "That's right. Werjes won't come anywhere near cheese of any kind, except perhaps American cheese, which has virtually no smell. It's the smell they hate."

"Victory city," the spiddles declared, hopping about in agitation. "A great, great day."

Nick said to his father, "Is there any sign of Horace?"

"I wasn't looking for Horace," his father said severely. "I was looking for you, Nick. You're a great deal more important."

"But we have to find him," Nick said.

"Let's go home first," his father replied. "You can rest up and I can finish talking to the police about Mr. Frankis. And then later, if we both feel well enough, and if it appears to be safe—"

Nick said, "Nothing is safe on this planet. Completely safe, I mean." There would always be Glimmung; there would always be werjes and trobes and, most awful of all, the father-things. That made him think, all at once, of what the nunk had told him. "The nunk which we ran into along the way—" he began, and then became silent. It would only worry his father, to tell him about the Nick-thing following along the road. And his father, as usual, was already worried enough.

"Yes," his father said. "What about the nunk?"

Nick said evasively, "Nunks are harmless. We met one along the way."

"I know they're harmless," his father replied in a worried voice. "Come on; let's get home." He started off in the direction from which they had come.

The uniformed man who had stood guard by the aged printer stopped Nick's father. "Mr. Graham," he said, "your son brought the first great true injury to Glimmung yet inflicted."

"Nick did?" his father asked. "Most amazing." He seemed a bit dazed. "I'm very glad," he said, but then, almost at once, he became worried again. "Weren't you taking a terrible chance, Nick?"

Nick sighed. "Yes," he admitted. "I was."

"But at least you're okay now," his father added. That cheered him up. Happily, he slapped Nick on the back. "So we've started out here in a positive way. This officer seems extremely proud of you."

The spiddles, collecting in a ring around Nick and his father, shouted in their clamorous voices, "Accomplishment city!"

"And the spiddles, too," the uniformed guard said. "They witnessed it. We all witnessed it. Glimmung will carry a phantom spear in his throat forever, because of what your boy has done. In his desolate, empty mountain places, Glimmung will nurse his unending wound and grow weaker day by day. He will grow bitter; he will brood and meditate. He will fade with each passing night. So you can understand why everyone is proud of your son."

That's fine, Nick thought to himself. But that didn't bring Horace back. Glumly, he followed after his father and Mr. McKenna as they began the journey back to the house.

The tireless spiddles came leaping along, too.

Chapter 17

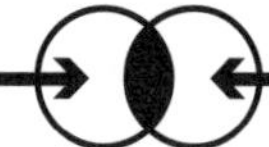

When they reached the place of slag and white rock, Nick's father and Mr. McKenna halted. Nick and the spiddles halted, too. For a long time they gazed at Glimmung's mark, the enormous cleft cut into the peak of the stark, rough hill. Each of them thought his private thoughts. No one spoke.

"He was here first, Glimmung was," a spiddle said at last, for the benefit of Nick's father and Mr. McKenna.

"I knew that already," Mr. McKenna said. "Everyone who lives on this world knows that." He had become grave and forbidding, as had Nick's father.

"Is he here now?" Nick's father asked the spiddles. "Did he come here again, after he was wounded?"

"Maybe," the spiddles chirped. They did not seem alarmed. "If so, he won't show himself."

They started on.

A far-off cry came to Nick. The cry drifted in the bleak air; it wavered, became faint, then louder again.

"Horace," Nick said. He could tell; he recognized the sound. At once he started from the path, stepping quickly over stones and the slab-like surfaces of once-molten slag. "I think it came from this direction," Nick said; he stumbled, then hurried on, climbing up the slope of the hill, towards Glimmung's mark.

His father shouted, "Nick! Stop! Don't go any further!" Both his father and Mr. McKenna yelled together.

"I'll be right back," Nick said, over his shoulder. Again he heard the cry. Again he knew it was Horace. The cat, lost somewhere in these lifeless hills...Horace would not survive long here. Nothing survived in this place, any more. Not since Glimmung had come.

Panting for breath, he halted briefly.

Above him, near Glimmung's mark, a black, small shape appeared. It paused there, uncertainly. It was Horace.

"Horace," Nick said, and again began to climb. He continued on, laboring and gasping; rocks tumbled about his feet, and once a massive section of lava broke off and crashed past him, to disappear below. The air became thick and difficult to breathe; it made him choke. Strange air, he said to himself wonderingly. As if fragments of dust inhabited it. He coughed, paused to get his breath, looked up the slope, trying to make out Horace.

The cat could still be seen. Horace stood on an outcropping of rock, perched there unsteadily. Again he cried out, and then, all at once, he disappeared. He had hopped down from the rock; he had gone on. Nick, wheezing, followed.

He came at last to a flat place, a kind of table of rock. From here he could see down in every direction. There, far below, stood his father and Mr. McKenna. And the spiddles. None of them, not even the faithful spiddles, had followed him this far. He was completely alone. The wind, cold and sparse, billowed about him; as it tugged at his shirt Nick felt even more alone. What an isolated place, he said to himself. So silent. So without life of any kind.

Directly above him, on a boulder, Horace appeared. The cat made no cry, this time; he merely stared down at Nick with his green, round eyes, his sewed-on, glass-button eyes which bulged, as usual, in awe. The cat was dusty; his black coat had become grey with coarse particles. And he looked very tired.

"Stay there," Nick said, and made his way carefully towards the rock. Reaching up, he tried to take hold of the cat. But Horace, for some obscure reason, moved backwards, away from Nick's grasping hands. "Please," Nick said. But the cat remained out of his reach. I'll have to climb higher, Nick realized. He found a ledge for his feet; hoisting himself up he again reached for the cat.

Horace had jumped down behind the boulder.

Gasping and winded, Nick managed to lift himself to the top. Now he saw down beyond the boulder; a sheltered place, small, where the wind did not blow. There Horace sat, an expression of bewilderment on his face. "You fool," Nick said pantingly. "All you have to do is walk towards me, just a few feet, and it will be over." We can go home, then, he thought. And rest. "Please," he said, reaching.

And then he saw the Nick-thing.

It stood just beyond Horace, not moving, not speaking. No wonder the cat did not know what to do. I and it, Nick said to himself. Identical. He felt terror. He gazed at the thing and it gazed back at him. A long time passed, or anyhow what seemed like a long time. And still the Nick-thing did not move. Yes, he thought; it's a father-thing; the one of me. Which got away, back near the house. The one the nunk warned us about. The one which followed me. Here it is. Waiting. It waited for me to come up here.

Horace walked back to the Nick-thing, as if to rub against its legs.

"No," Nick said sharply.

The cat hesitated. He started away from the Nick-thing, then stopped.

The Nick-thing bent down and said, "Horace."

Quickly, the cat hurried over to it.

I've lost him, Nick said to himself. He watched the Nick-thing pick up Horace; he watched it stand erect, holding Horace in its arms and stroking him.

"Give me back my cat," Nick said.

The Nick-thing continued to hold Horace.

"I want him back," Nick said. "He belongs to me, not to you. Can I have him now?" He waited.

Lifting Horace, the Nick-thing held the cat out.

"Thanks," Nick said. He reached down and took the cat from the Nick-thing's arms. The Nick-thing smiled a little; a wistful, wan smile. Then it turned and walked away. Nick, holding Horace tightly, watched it go.

"Miaow," Horace said plaintively.

Step by step, Nick climbed back down the rocky hill, back to the path where his father and Mr. McKenna and the spiddles waited. They had not seen the Nick-thing. Only he, himself, knew about it. And Horace, too; Horace had seen it. But the cat did not understand, so that did not count.

"Are you all right?" his father asked.

"Yes." Nick nodded. "Fine."

"Let's get out of these hills," his father said. "They worry me. I'll feel better when we get home." He started off; Nick and Mr. McKenna and the spiddles followed.

Horace, in Nick's arms, rubbed and purred. "It's good to have you back," Nick said to him. The cat bumped his face against Nick's chin, showing his pleasure at finding Nick again. "I'll bet you really bit the two trobes who ran off with you," Nick said. "Didn't you?" The cat, as if agreeing, continued to rub. He seemed self-satisfied, as if he had done a noble thing. "Yes," Nick said. "You did."

Looking back, Nick tried to catch sight of the Nick-thing. It had not followed.

"Safety city," one of the spiddles piped.

And so it was.